P9-DCC-477

Emma was more frightened than she'd ever been in her life.

Her memory was spotty at best. She was filling in the edges, but a giant blank space remained at the center. The blow to her head had left her with only random dribbles of recollection surrounding the events leading to the accident.

Who had put the envelope of photos in her overnight bag—and when? They'd been placed there after the accident, that much she knew.

Someone had been watching her and wanted her to know she was exposed.

"I'm sorry," Liam said, his expression awash with guilt. "We were supposed to keep you safe, and we didn't."

"I don't blame you. Everyone did their best. I'm here, aren't I? I survived the accident. I survived the attack."

She'd survived because someone out there wanted her to. He wanted her alive because he had worse things in store for her.

Her stalker was giving her sly nudges to let her know she wasn't safe. He was letting her know there were *no* gaps in *his* memory of her.

Sherri Shackelford is an award-winning author of inspirational books featuring ordinary people discovering extraordinary love. A reformed pessimist, Sherri has a passion for storytelling. Her books are fast paced and heartfelt with a generous dose of humor. She loves to hear from readers at sherri@sherrishackelford.com. Visit her website at sherrishackelford.com.

Visit the Author Profile page at Harlequin.com for more titles.

KILLER AMNESIA

SHERRI SHACKELFORD

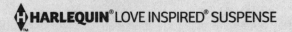
HARLEQUIN®LOVE INSPIRED® SUSPENSE

If you purchased this book without a cover you should be aware
that this book is stolen property. It was reported as "unsold and
destroyed" to the publisher, and neither the author nor the
publisher has received any payment for this "stripped book."

Recycling programs
for this product may
not exist in your area.

LOVE INSPIRED BOOKS

ISBN-13: 978-1-335-23241-0

Killer Amnesia

Copyright © 2019 by Sherri Shackelford

All rights reserved. Except for use in any review, the reproduction
or utilization of this work in whole or in part in any form by any
electronic, mechanical or other means, now known or hereafter
invented, including xerography, photocopying and recording, or in
any information storage or retrieval system, is forbidden without
the written permission of the editorial office, Love Inspired Books,
195 Broadway, New York, NY 10007 U.S.A.

This is a work of fiction. Names, characters, places and incidents are
either the product of the author's imagination or are used fictitiously, and
any resemblance to actual persons, living or dead, business establishments,
events or locales is entirely coincidental.

This edition published by arrangement with Love Inspired Books.

® and TM are trademarks of Love Inspired Books, used under license.
Trademarks indicated with ® are registered in the United States Patent
and Trademark Office, the Canadian Intellectual Property Office and in
other countries.

www.Harlequin.com

Printed in U.S.A.

Create in me a clean heart, O God;
and renew a right spirit within me.
—Psalm 51:10

To the people who stay up later than they should to read the next page, to the people who can immediately flip to their favorite scene in their favorite book, to the people who save the last page until the next day because they're not quite ready to let go of their new friends...
To all the readers in the world, thank you!
The laundry can wait; it's time for an adventure.

ONE

Deputy Liam McCallister was a dead man.

At least that's what everyone back in Dallas thought. Until six months ago, he was working undercover in the Gang Unit of the Dallas Police Department. Now he was stuck in a small town directing traffic under the name Deputy McCourt. At least the US Marshals had assigned him a job in law enforcement while the district attorney wrapped up the case. They figured he was safe as long as he kept a low profile. No one from the Serpent Brotherhood would be caught dead in Redbird, Texas.

The irony wasn't lost on him.

If the Serpent Brotherhood knew they'd been infiltrated, they'd shut down their operations. This was better. Except one month had turned into six without a break in the case, and the wait was starting to get to him.

Fighting his way through the pelting downpour, Liam adjusted the flashing yellow barricades and ducked into his state-issue Chevy Tahoe. Heavy rains had washed out the road. There was no escaping Redbird, Texas, tonight.

A shock of static sounded from his police radio, and a familiar voice filled the cab.

"Unit 120," Rose Johnson, the dispatcher, called.

Soaking wind slapped against his windshield in pounding bursts. Lightning streaked across the black sky, temporarily illuminating a bank of angry clouds.

Liam grasped the microphone and depressed the Call button. "Unit 120."

"Single car accident on Highway 214," the dispatcher relayed. "Personal injury. Mile-marker 37. Just beyond Brown Cattle feeders. Unit 130 is on scene. Requesting assistance. Fire and rescue en route."

"Ten-four. Responding from County Road 12."

Exhaustion rippled through him. He was working a double shift that had started before six this morning. Only the county sheriff along with two deputies were assigned to this area, and the three of them were spread thin.

He flipped on his flashing red lights and pulled a U-turn. A canine whimper sounded from the backseat, and Liam glanced over his shoulder. "Sorry, Duchess, looks like you're stuck with me."

He'd discovered the animal earlier in the day wandering around the town square. The tag listed her name but no phone number. A nuisance call and a traffic stop had prevented him from reaching the county shelter before closing. Though bedraggled from being caught in the rain, the dog was well fed—too well fed. Someone must be worried about her.

He handed over a bone-shaped biscuit from the box he'd purchased earlier. "Why are you complaining? You'll be home before me at this rate."

Soon the flashing lights of Deputy Jim Bishop's identical Chevy Tahoe appeared, and Liam eased his vehicle to the side of the road.

His radio popped to life. "Unit 120." Rose's voice was solemn. "Deputy Bishop called in a code four."

A frisson went through him.

All the years he'd been in law enforcement, he'd yet to overcome his latent dread of fatality calls. "Ten-four."

He adjusted the collar of his slicker, tugged his hat

lower over his forehead and stepped into the pouring rain. Splashing through ankle-deep puddles, he jogged the distance to where Deputy Bishop stood vigil.

Tall and gaunt with thinning sand-colored hair, Bishop was openly gunning for the sheriff's job in the next election. Given what Liam had seen of the deputy's job performance, the guy had a better chance of getting kicked by a snake.

The man pointed a slender arm. "Down there. Got a brief look at her before the rising water drove me back."

A beige Fiat 500 rested upright in water from the culvert, rain streaming through the shattered sunroof. Liam recognized the car—the model was distinctive—but he didn't know the driver.

"Single fatality," Deputy Bishop shouted over the storm. "Female."

Judging by the crumpled exterior, the car had rolled at least once before landing at the bottom of the ditch. The headlights cast a weak, shimmering beam through the rising water, and Liam caught a glimpse of the motionless driver.

"Any identification?" Liam asked.

"Rose is running the license plates."

Liam always trusted that God had a plan. Sometimes that plan was human intervention. "I'll check it out."

"You can't. You'll be washed away by the current."

"Turn on your searchlights," Liam called over his shoulder.

He shucked his utility belt but kept his police two-way radio clipped to his shirt collar. Rummaging through the rear compartment of his vehicle, he retrieved a rope, then slammed the hatch shut. He paused a moment before deciding to forgo the backboard. Fire and rescue were better equipped to retrieve the body.

Bishop's truck was parked with the nose angled toward the ditch. After securing the rope to the bumper, Liam tied off and backed toward the vertical grade.

"Take up the slack," he called.

Bishop nodded.

The drop wasn't far, but it was steep. Liam's boots sank into the muddy embankment, and his arms strained against holding the bulk of his weight. Moisture had already soaked through his collar and saturated his uniform. Though it was early spring, the rain was just shy of sleet. He could have left his slicker behind for all the good it was doing him.

His gloved hands slipped, and he lost his grip. The slack broke free. He plunged the last few feet into icy, calf-deep water, his hip bumping painfully into the car's rear fender. Stumbling and slipping, he managed to fight the current.

"Thanks for keeping the slack, Bishop," he mumbled darkly.

His feet went numb almost immediately. The rain was coming down too fast, turning runoff from the culvert into a shallow, raging river. The water reached his knees and wrenched at his balance. Gripping the car roof for purchase, he squinted through the dim glow of Bishop's searchlights and wrestled his way to the shattered driver's window.

Submerged to the waist, the woman's lifeless body was slumped over the deployed airbag. Her right arm bobbed near the gearshift, palm up, the fingers curled, and her dark hair hung limply around her downturned face. Papers drifted in the current, escaping through the broken passenger window.

Liam's throat tightened. Even without seeing her face, he sensed she was about his age.

He offered a brief prayer for her and the family she left behind.

Taking a deep, steadying breath, he grasped her shoulder and pulled her upright. Her head lolled backward, and her dark hair plastered wetly across her ashen cheeks. He aimed the beam of his flashlight toward her face. Blood oozed from a gash near her temple, and a purple bruise darkened one eye.

He brushed her hair aside. There was something familiar about her, but he couldn't place where he'd seen her before. Maybe he'd stood behind her in line at the supermarket. A likely occurrence in a town the size of Redbird.

Her eyes flew open.

Adrenaline spiked through his veins, and the flashlight slipped from his fingers. She gulped for air, her chest heaving, then feebly groped the front of his coat, her expression panicked.

"H-help me."

He'd caught a brief glimpse of her eyes. A unique shade of amber topaz.

Catching the woman's hands, he pressed them between his gloves. She wasn't dead, but she was going to be if they didn't get her out of this water soon.

"It's all right," he soothed. "Fire and rescue are on the way."

"Wh-who are you?" Her teeth chattered.

The question caught him off guard for a moment. That was the problem with being a dead man—remembering his cover name didn't always come easy.

He sluiced the moisture from his face. "I'm Deputy Liam McCourt with the county sheriff's department. What's your name, ma'am?"

"My name is..." An expression of abject terror descended over her features. "I don't know. I d-don't know what my name is! Wh-what's happening to me?"

A fresh sense of urgency filled him. Injuries from car accidents were notoriously deceptive.

"It's all right." He cupped his hand behind her head, and she turned her face into his palm. "Don't be afraid."

He caught sight of Bishop's silhouette outlined by the searchlights and depressed the button on his two-way. "Check on fire and rescue. They're late."

"I'm c-cold," she managed to say between chattering teeth.

Something wasn't right. People sometimes forgot the events leading up to an accident, as though the trauma bleached their memories, but he'd never encountered someone who'd forgotten their own name.

"Don't worry," he said. "We'll get you out of here."

"Promise?" She clutched the lapel of his jacket. "Please don't lie to me."

Don't lie to me.

The past six months melted away, and he was no longer standing in the freezing rain. He was suffocating in the sweltering Dallas heat. His memory had taken him to when he was working undercover in the Serpent Brotherhood, playing the same game he'd perfected in foster care. He was pretending to fit in. Pretending to be something he wasn't. Not even Jenny had seen through his act, and they'd briefly attended grade school together.

For once Liam had been grateful the foster system had bounced him from family to family. Jenny hadn't known he'd gone to college before joining the Dallas PD. The few people who remembered him from those days believed he was just another kid from the old neighborhood—all grown up and going nowhere.

Are you a cop? Don't lie to me. Jenny's words echoed

in his mind. Her boyfriend, Swerve, was the lead fixer in the gang and took care of problems by making them disappear. Swerve was responsible for more than one missing person in the Dallas area. He'd gotten agitated during the exchange, and he'd accidentally pulled the trigger. The bullet had carved a path through Liam's left shoulder, shattering his clavicle before slicing into Jenny's neck. She'd bled out before the paramedics had arrived.

The scene was a mess, and Swerve thought he'd killed them both. The US Marshals had done the rest. They'd given Liam a new last name and tucked him away while the case wove its slow path through the court system.

A broken tree limb slammed into Liam's shin, ripping his feet from beneath him, forcing him back to the present. He caught hold of the door handle and dragged himself upright, then wrapped his arm through the open window, bracing his body. A sharp metal edge dug painfully through his sleeve.

"Are you hurt anywhere else?" Keeping her head supported with one hand, he gently touched the lump on her forehead. "Can you tell if anything is broken?"

"I d-don't k-know. I don't th-think so." She frantically beat against the water swirling around her waist. "I have to get out of here."

"Soon." He depressed the Call button on his radio and leaned his ear to his shoulder. "Where's that fire truck?"

A grating voice sounded from the microphone attached to Liam's collar. "Delayed. Driver didn't know the road was washed out."

"Tell 'em it's urgent."

"Hold your horses. Not gonna change things for the victim."

"She's alive, Bishop."

The momentary shock of silence was deafening. "That can't be. I checked. I didn't feel a pulse."

No use arguing about the details when there was a life hanging in the balance. Who knew what other injuries she might have sustained, and she was at risk for hypothermia.

"There's a backboard in my truck. Send it down," Liam ordered.

"Ten-four," came the quiet reply.

The car lurched against the tide of rainwater, and his heart slammed against his ribs.

She didn't have time to wait for fire and rescue. "We're getting you out of here, ma'am, but you'll have to work with me. Can you do that?"

He risked exacerbating her injuries by moving her, but she was going to drown otherwise.

She gave a hesitant nod. The car shifted again, and she bolted upright, grasping his arm.

"Yes," she gasped. "H-help me."

His shoulder protested the abuse, and he grimaced.

The woman stilled. "What's wrong? Are y-you all right?"

"It's nothing," he replied gruffly.

His feet sank deeper into the mud, and his gut churned. He didn't know how much longer he could keep his footing. He didn't know how much longer they had before the water swept away the car.

The woman took another deep, gulping breath. "I trust you."

Her declaration knocked the breath from his lungs. The last person who'd trusted him, Jenny, had paid the ultimate price. He'd prayed to God plenty growing up, especially during the worst times, and he'd begged God to save Jenny that day.

He'd gotten the same answer he'd grown accustomed to: silence.

He didn't resent God for ignoring his prayers, instead, he'd learned that if a man never asked for anything, he was never disappointed.

Lightning streaked across the sky. Thunder rattled the shattered windshield, and her grip on his arm tightened. His past no longer mattered. What mattered now was this woman's safety.

"Someone f-forced me off the road," she said. "S-someone tried to kill me."

She found herself in a freezing nightmare of throbbing pain. Blood pounded inside her skull. Her other pains were too numerous to count, and the frigid rain had her bones aching.

The water was rising.

Her heart hammered against her ribs. She wasn't staying in this car another minute.

"Did you hear me?" She tried to shout over the rushing water, but the words came out warbled. "About the accident?"

"I heard you," the deputy said, a reassuring hand on her shoulder. "I'll get a description of the vehicle and the driver once you're squared away."

"A t-truck, I th-think."

She attempted to reconstruct the moments before careening off the road, but the images at the edges of her vision blurred.

Someone had tried to kill her, and they'd nearly succeeded.

Her eyes must have drifted shut, because the next instant, Deputy McCourt was gently nudging her. "Stay with me."

He was somewhere in his early thirties and handsome

in an earnestly boyish kind of way. The weak beam of light from the highway above wasn't strong enough to see his eyes, but she had a vague impression they were blue. His beard was dark, and she assumed the hair beneath his brimmed hat matched. He was tall—his shape hidden beneath his enveloping slicker.

The car shifted, and she frantically reached beneath the water to unfasten her seat belt. The mechanism released, and the sudden freedom sent pain shooting through her shoulder.

She clutched her upper arm and groaned.

"What's wrong?" The deputy steadied her through the broken window. "What happened?"

The strap had been cutting into her collarbone, but she'd been too preoccupied by everything else to notice. "I'm f-fine. Just the seat belt."

Her lips were going numb, making speech difficult. She pressed her palm against her throbbing head and winced.

The deputy broke the few remaining glass shards from the surrounding window frame. "You'll have to crawl out. I'll help you."

"A-all right."

As she drifted in and out of consciousness, the next few minutes passed in a blur. Strong arms lifted her from the car's wreckage. The pain came in gasping waves. Even the slightest movement jolted her battered limbs. Once the deputy had positioned her on the backboard, she struggled feebly against his insistence on checking her for additional injuries. She was fine. She could walk. As he secured her upper body, a shaft of pure agony jerked through her.

"Sorry," the deputy mumbled. "You have a dislocated shoulder."

She blinked rapidly through the rain streaming over her face. "Can you put it back?"

"Take a deep breath." He hovered over her, his gaze intense. "This is gonna hurt."

His sharp movement caused an anguished cry, but the relief was almost immediate.

"You're right," she gasped. "That hurt."

At least she'd learned one thing about herself—she appreciated honesty.

He brushed the back of his gloved hand over her temple. "Sorry."

Stepping away, he slipped out of his raincoat.

She held up a restraining hand. "I'm already soaked. Y-you need that more than I do."

"No arguments." He leaned over her, adjusting the ties near her head, his body shielding her from the worst of the rain. "You can at least pretend like I'm in charge, ma'am."

"Don't call me ma'am," she said weakly, wondering if he'd even hear her words over the rain. "Makes me feel old."

His expression shifted. "What else should I call you?"

She probed the edges of her memory but met only an endless blank wall.

A sudden terror took hold, as though she was standing on the edge of a void. Her lungs constricted, and she couldn't breathe. She desperately searched for something that made sense. She knew the man standing above her was a deputy. She recognized the insignia on his hat. Clinging to that one simple fact, she inhaled deeply. If she followed familiar items, they'd lead her out of this shadowy maze.

He clasped her hand. "Never mind. Don't try and remember. We'll stick with ma'am for now."

The deputy made a signal with his hand and the backboard heaved. She grimaced, attempting to hide her discomfort.

"You're doing great," he said, his face a blur in the falling rain. "Not much longer."

"I don't have anything else planned."

He grinned. "Keep that sense of humor."

Images raced through her head. She recalled the steady swish of the windshield wipers—the crash of thunder. The visions were like memories from a dream—hazy and unfocused. Had she imagined the whole thing? She couldn't have. There'd been a white pickup truck. The driver had crossed in front of her, striking her driver's-side bumper. The blow had sent her car tumbling. The glass around her had shattered.

Then—nothing.

Her pulse sputtered. That was the worst part—the nothing. The nothing was horrifying. When she neared the edge of her memories, her stomach dropped as though she was falling. As though she was dropping into an endless void.

The only thing she knew for certain was the shocking feel of her car rolling down the hill, and the deputy's soothing voice. Everything else was gone.

Erased.

When they neared the top of the embankment, another deputy joined them. He was older. Thinner. Not as handsome as Deputy McCourt, and his expression was stricken. Did she really look that bad? The two men rapidly unfastened her from the backboard, and the second man reached for her.

She frantically clutched Deputy McCourt's arm. "No."

The reaction came from a gut instinct she didn't understand and couldn't govern. Uncontrollable trembling seized her body, and her teeth chattered.

"You drive, Bishop," Deputy McCourt ordered. "We'll take my truck."

He gathered her in his arms, compressing her shaking limbs. He was the only solid thing in her world, the only person she remembered. She pressed her cheek into the damp material of his shirt, her mind filling in the blank spaces with impressions of him. His deep, baritone voice, the curve of his lips in a half smile, the feel of his rough beard against her cheek as he'd drawn her close.

"I'm s-so cold," she murmured, her mouth close to his ear.

The next moment the rain ceased pounding her skin, and a door slammed. She gasped in sheer relief. The noises outside were instantly muffled, soothing even. She was sheltered. She was safe. Reckless gratitude flooded through her, and she never wanted to leave the protection of the deputy's arms. His strength and self-assurance were comforting. Everything outside the circle was unknown.

"Not much longer," he said, his warm breath a soothing balm against her chilled skin. "Stay with me."

"T-tell me your name again," she pleaded, her voice hoarse. "Y-your first n-name."

For reasons she couldn't explain, his brief hesitation alarmed her.

"Liam. My name is Liam."

She sensed his ambivalence toward her. As though he didn't want to be kind to her but couldn't find it in his nature to act unkind.

"Liam," she repeated, testing the name on her tongue, but there was no spark of familiarity. "Do I know you?"

"I don't think so, ma'am, but I haven't lived in town long."

Panic threatened to crush her. How much had she forgotten? What if she was imprisoned in this vacant place forever?

Her breath came in shallow puffs. The memory flashed in her mind again. A white truck. The crash of steel on steel. The sound of breaking glass. Then…nothing.

As though familiar with her moods, Liam seemed to sense the moment the wave of anxiety threatened to drown her.

"You're all right," he soothed. "The doc at the ER is

good. He's reliable. I've never seen his car parked outside Red's Bar and Grill. That's something around here. Not much else to do."

The even drone of his voice steadied her. She couldn't look backward; she had to look forward.

Something touched her elbow and she started.

Liam chuckled. "Don't worry. She's harmless. She's my unofficial deputy today. Say hello, Duchess."

The muzzle of a rust-colored Pomeranian nuzzled her arm, provoking a reluctant grin.

A staticky voice sounded over the police radio. "I have a positive ID on the license plates," the voice declared.

"Go ahead," the deputy who was driving said.

She was breathless, her heart pounding as though she was standing on the edge of a precipice. If the dispatcher said her name, surely there'd be a spark of recognition.

"The car is registered to a female. Brown eyes. Brown hair. Five feet five inches, one hundred and thirty pounds, age twenty-nine. Initial background check has her occupation listed as self-employed. Journalist. The name is Emma Lyons."

Nothing. No flash of memory. No spark of recognition. Nothing. Her stomach pitched, and her fragile world collapsed.

Someone wanted Emma Lyons dead.

Someone wanted *her* dead.

Why?

TWO

After briefly going home to change into a dry uniform, Liam pushed through the double doors separating the hospital emergency room area from the patient wing, then followed the room numbers. Plastic sheeting blocked the far end of the hallway.

The hospital was in the middle of a long-overdue renovation to keep pace with a new facility in the next town over.

Running his finger beneath the collar of his uniform shirt, Liam strode down the corridor. He'd wrap up his end of the investigation and leave the rest to Bishop. End of story. This was no time to become entangled in something personal, and he was drawn to Emma. The combination was toxic.

She was standing beside the bed in a shapeless, blue-patterned hospital gown, her arm in a sling. Her damp hair was freshly brushed and hung in a chestnut curtain brushing her shoulders.

She appeared lost and alone, and his decision to remain impartial faltered. His name might be a lie and the job might be temporary, but he had eight years of law enforcement experience behind him. His expertise hadn't deserted him even if his name and his job title were different.

Despite the purple bruising and stitches around her temple, Emma Lyons was pretty in a fresh, hometown-girl sort of way. Though not very tall, she was athletically built. No spouse or children had come up on her background check, and Rose was searching for an emergency contact.

She took a wobbly step forward, her good arm outstretched for balance.

He rushed to her side. "Are you supposed to be out of bed?"

"Sorry." She swayed into him. "Just a little dizzier than I thought."

He instinctively wrapped his arm around her waist. Her smile of thanks was radiant, and warmth spread up his neck. They stood close enough that he noted the pale freckles sprinkled flirtatiously across the bridge of her nose.

He snuck a glance at her face. "All right?"

"Better, thank you."

An unexpected shock of awareness rippled across his heart. Clutching his forearms, she dropped wearily onto the hospital bed and exhaled, her cheeks puffing.

A dark-skinned man in scrubs and a lab coat stepped into the room.

Liam backed away, bumping into the edge of the bed frame. "She, uh, needed some help."

The doctor was in his late forties with black hair and an empathetic smile.

"I'm Dr. Javadi," he said. "We spoke earlier. Will Deputy Bishop be joining us?"

"He's still on scene," Liam replied.

And none too happy about it. Bishop was knee-deep in mud when Liam drove by on the way back to the hospital. The deputy had been too bored to stick around the ER, but he was most likely regretting his decision to leave.

"Right," the doctor said. "Any change in your condition, Ms. Lyons?"

"I was looking at myself in the mirror," Emma said with a sigh. "Do you know what it's like, staring at a stranger?"

The doctor retrieved a computer tablet from a large, square pocket on his lab coat. "Considering what Deputy McCourt told me about the accident, you're incredibly fortunate, Ms. Lyons. You've suffered various scrapes and bruises along with a dislocated shoulder."

He turned to Liam. "Were you the one who set that?"

"I made the call on scene."

"You did the right thing," the doctor replied brusquely. "Being young and healthy, you should recover quickly, Ms. Lyons."

Emma made a sound of frustration. "I'm well aware of my physical injuries. What's wrong with my head? Why can't I remember my name? My address? Where am I, anyway?"

Liam's attention sharpened. He'd assumed her earlier confusion was temporary.

"We're in Redbird, Texas," he offered.

She lifted her arm, her fingers fluttering. "That means nothing to me."

Battling temptation, he remained silent—offering no words of comfort. Jenny had seen him as something he wasn't. The betrayal in her eyes when she'd taken her last breath was seared on his soul. He couldn't risk getting too close to a victim in a case while he was living a lie. He couldn't afford to blur the lines with Emma.

"You're suffering from an atypical form of retrograde amnesia," Dr. Javadi said, his voice gratingly patient. "Though rare, it's not an unheard-of condition."

Emma pressed the heels of her hands against her temples. "I don't understand."

"Retrograde amnesia tends to affect autobiographical memory but leaves procedural memory in place."

The two men remained silent, letting her absorb the information. Emotions flitted across her expressive face: fear, confusion…annoyance.

Her hands dropped to her sides, leaving an angry splash of red where she'd been pressing. "You're saying that even though I don't know my name, I can tie my shoes and tell the time. That's why you had me do all those things before, isn't it?"

"Exactly. As long as you possessed a skill before the accident, you'll have that same skill now."

"I thought that sort of thing only happened in movies."

The doctor flashed a weak smile. "Reality is often stranger than fiction."

"What's the cure?" Emma adjusted her shoulder sling with a grimace. "Is there something familiar I can look at? Someone I can call who will jog my memory?"

Liam's heart went out to her. He knew a little something about being a stranger in a strange place. She was vulnerable, and for reasons he couldn't explain, he was protective of her.

"Reminder treatment has proven unreliable in these cases," the doctor said. "In all likelihood, you'll recover your memory, although the time around the accident may never come back. We don't have a lot of studies on the subject, but experience has taught us that the memories surrounding a trauma are the most fragile. On the plus side, these cases generally resolve themselves when swelling in the temporal lobe abates. You may experience a spontaneous recovery, or your memory may come back in pieces, in random order. There are no guarantees, though.

The episode may last days or even weeks. In extremely rare cases, the damage can be permanent."

"No." Emma blinked rapidly, her eyes welling with tears. "No. This isn't permanent. I won't believe that. I can't believe that."

Liam staggered back a step. *Permanent?*

She scooted nearer and grasped his sleeve, her gaze imploring. At his brief hesitation, hurt flickered across her topaz eyes, and she looked away. She was attempting to put on a brave face and mostly succeeding.

While he longed to rest a comforting hand on her shoulder—to offer some sort of gesture to make her feel less alone— he couldn't. He'd learned his lesson the hard way. When emotions ran high, even the slightest gesture was liable to be misconstrued.

Clearing his throat, he said, "We'll contact your family. You shouldn't be alone."

"My family?" Her eyes widened. "Do I have a husband? Children?"

"No spouse or children came up in the initial background check," Liam said quickly over her panic. "You're self-employed, which means we haven't been able to locate an emergency contact."

The doctor retrieved a stylus from his scrubs pocket and scribbled something on the tablet screen. "I'm keeping you a few days for observation."

Emma's jaw dropped and quickly snapped shut again. "I'm perfectly capable of taking care of myself."

"I know," the doctor said quietly. "But considering your condition, I can't, in good conscience, release you. Think of your brain like an engine. This injury has run you out of gas. The only way to refuel is with rest."

"An engine?" She harrumphed. "I feel like I've been in

a demolition derby. And what about my car? I'm assuming I won't be able to drive it anytime soon."

"More like never." Liam speared a hand through his damp hair. "The car is totaled. We'll retrieve your personal effects and have it towed to the county impound while we investigate the accident."

"What about my parents? Siblings?" she asked, a quiver at the end of her question. "Is anyone looking for me?"

"Your parents are deceased," Liam said. There was nothing that might indicate her location on the internet— her address had been removed from all the usual locations, and even those databases that were less familiar to laymen, as though she was hiding from something. *Or someone.* "The closest relative is listed as a brother. We're tracking him down. I'm not concerned we haven't received a call about a missing person. People tend to drift off schedule over the weekend. Come Monday, we'll probably get a hit."

Emma blinked rapidly, a myriad of emotions flitting across her eloquent features, and he wanted to kick himself. This case was different. She wasn't the usual victim. Everything was foreign to her. Hearing the details of her life was like learning of her parents' deaths for the first time.

The doctor shot him a quelling glance. "You've had an eventful day, Ms. Lyons. It's late. A lot of these details can wait until the morning. I'll want to speak with you before she's released, Deputy McCourt."

Liam gave a negative shake of his head. "Deputy Bishop is the lead on this case."

"I'd rather work with you." Emma reached for him. "Do I have any say in the matter?"

Fighting his better nature, he avoided her appeal. He was tired of living in limbo. Each day he was away from

Dallas, he slipped further from his old life. If he accepted this assignment, he risked being torn between two responsibilities. The US Marshals were liable to call him back to testify any day now. He had no business digging into a troublesome and personal case when he might not be able to follow through.

"Deputy Bishop was the first on scene," Liam said. "It's up to the sheriff to change the assignments."

His protective feelings for Emma didn't play any part in the matter. Emotions were a luxury he couldn't afford.

"You didn't leave me before," she pleaded. "You can't abandon me now."

A swelling pulse throbbed in his ears. His first partner had nicknamed him "The Pitbull" because once he got his teeth into a case, he locked his jaws and didn't let go. Despite his personal doubts, he'd gone along with faking his death. The department and the Feds had invested too much time and too many resources to risk blowing the case.

No matter the reasons, whether real or fake, his death had left unfinished business. If God didn't answer prayers from guys like Liam, then he had to do the work himself. No amount of righteous conviction assuaged his guilt.

"We'll assess your situation in the morning." The doctor spoke into the awkward silence. "For now, get some rest, Ms. Lyons. The staff can reach me if there's a change in your condition." He paused in the doorway. "I'll call the sheriff's office when the rest of the tox reports come back."

Liam had hauled in enough drunk drivers to know the tests would come back negative. "Sure."

There was white paint on the bumper of Emma's car, corroborating her story that someone had forced her off the road.

Bishop had labeled the case an aggravated assault with a motor vehicle—no credible leads. Given her loss of memory, they were starting from scratch. There was no immediate way of knowing if Emma had a jealous boyfriend or a disgruntled acquaintance in her past.

The lengths she'd gone to in order to hide her address on the internet gave the only hint there might be someone out there who wanted to harm her. People who simply preferred to remain anonymous online generally didn't have the resources for such a thorough internet cleaning of location information. Then again, maybe she was simply a private person who was willing to pay to stay off the grid.

She glanced at her clenched hands. "I'm scared."

Her whispered confession tugged at his conscience. "There's a security guard, Tim, who we keep on call for… unique situations." Usually for the unruly drunks being treated after a bar fight. He glanced at the clock. Nearly midnight. "I've got some paperwork to fill out. I might as well wait around for him. I'll be just outside the door if you need anything."

He desperately craved some shut-eye, but her vulnerability kept him rooted in place. There was no harm in sticking around a little while longer.

"I appreciate the offer." She managed a wobbly half smile. "But it's late. You should go home to your family."

"Don't worry. There's no one waiting up for me." He mentally chastised himself for the lapse. Why had he offered up that information? "Try and get some sleep."

She leaned to the side, pulling her legs to rest on the bed. After adjusting her pillow, she tucked one hand beneath her cheek. "Thank you for saving me tonight."

The blanket was trapped beneath her injured arm. He carefully dislodged the edge and draped the material around her shoulders. Avoiding her gaze, he shuffled back a few steps. His fingers itched to brush the hair from her forehead, but he caught himself just in time. What was wrong with him? Lack of sleep was turning him sentimental.

He wasn't a nurturing person. He never had been. Maybe if he'd been raised differently…or maybe not. Maybe he simply wasn't wired that way.

"I'd do the same for anyone," he said, wincing at the harsh edge in his tone. "It's part of the job."

There was no need to make this personal. His involvement was already drifting into a gray area. Bishop was the first responder on scene. The investigation wasn't Liam's responsibility unless the sheriff said otherwise.

She offered another smile that sent heat curling through his stomach.

"I'm sorry for all the trouble," she said, her hand muffling a yawn. "I'm sure this wasn't how you planned to spend your evening."

She was grateful to him, but gratitude went only so far. He wasn't the sort of guy who women introduced to mom and dad. His past was a hinderance.

Marrying someone meant marrying their family, as well, and no one wanted to marry into the mess that was his family tree.

He stared at the tops of his scuffed boots. "Deputy Bishop will update you on the case when he has more information."

A muscle twitched in his jaw. He wasn't abandoning her. He'd keep an eye on Bishop's handling of the investigation. He always did.

When she awkwardly reached to adjust the blanket, he kept his hands at his sides.

"Will I see you again?" she asked quietly.

"Probably not."

If the doctor was right, she'd most likely wake with total recall. Once she remembered who wanted to harm her, even Bishop couldn't botch the case, saving Liam from any further involvement.

"Good night, Emma."

"Good night," she managed to say over another sleepy yawn.

No loose ends. No regrets.

Why, then, did he feel as though it was already too late for both of them?

Emma startled awake and glanced at the clock in sleepy confusion. Just before 6:00 a.m. Which meant…she bolted upright. Today was Sunday already. After the accident on Friday evening, Saturday had passed in a blur. She'd slept nearly the entire day and night.

Her impressions of the time were hazy. Nurses had told her to rest, but each time she'd dozed, she'd returned to the nightmare of the crash and the water rising around her. They'd finally convinced her to take something to sleep, and she'd spent the rest of the evening in blissful oblivion.

They were planning on sending her home today—whatever that meant—and she was terrified.

She'd been avoiding the shadowy recesses of her brain, fearful of the accompanying panic. Daybreak had brought a reckoning. She'd have to re-create her past brushstroke by brushstroke, no matter what lay hidden in the shadows.

Lightning temporarily illuminated the room, a harbinger of the windowpane-rattling clap of thunder.

She thought of Deputy McCourt, and despair jolted through her. She trusted him more than the other deputy, the one who'd left her in the watery nightmare, but Liam had been emphatic about his limited involvement in the case.

She'd have to rely on herself, and that meant finding out who wanted her dead.

Trembling with anticipation, she tossed off the blankets. She was wide awake and desperate for coffee. Maybe she'd take the opportunity to walk the corridors and stretch her legs. A stack of folded clothing rested on the chair beside her bed.

Her shoulder was stiff and sore, but she didn't need the sling. One of the hospital staff had washed her sleeveless blue shell top, thin navy cardigan and jeans. Her tennis shoes were stiff from the dried rain, but she managed to untangle the laces and slide them on.

She caught sight of her reflection in the mirror and started. Approaching the glass, she touched her cheek with quaking fingers. Her heartbeat picked up rhythm and her breathing grew shallow. She'd seen her face in the mirror before, but she was still growing accustomed to the sight. As though she was looking at someone else through the reflection.

Wrenching her gaze away, she sucked in a deep, calming breath.

She had to get out of this room—out of her head—if only for a moment.

Tim, the security guard, was sprawled on a chair outside her room with his arms crossed and his chin tucked against his chest as he snored softly. Emma grimaced. Not exactly the protection she was offered, but given the state of her memory, she understood the skepticism about her claims.

Deputy Bishop had spoken to her only briefly. He'd dropped off the personal possessions from her car and asked a few perfunctory questions about her recollection of events.

She hadn't been sorry to see him go.

An empty cup of coffee rested near Tim's foot, and her annoyance dissipated. He'd kept watch over her two nights in a row. No wonder he was tired. She'd make some noise on her return to wake him.

A fresh-faced nurse in navy scrubs decorated with cartoon kittens directed her to an employee break room at the far end of the building—the only source of coffee that didn't involve anxious grandparents waiting on an expectant mother in labor and delivery. The hospital was too small for a cafeteria.

Following the nurse's directions, she maneuvered through the overlapping plastic sheeting separating the renovations from the occupied areas of the hospital. There were four additional patient rooms, two on either side of the corridor. The first door was propped open, and she caught sight of the gutted space with bare Sheetrock walls and colorful wires dangling from the ceiling.

The combined scents of paint and sawdust triggered a sense of familiarity, sparking a memory that was just out of reach.

She pressed her fists against her temples, willing the image to take shape.

Nothing.

Her head pounded from the futile effort, and she dropped her hands to her sides. Her brain might as well be this deserted wing of this hospital—empty, under construction and full of obstacles.

She took a step, and her toe caught on a stack of ceiling tiles. Yelping, she stumbled to the side, then stifled her amplified reaction with a hand to her mouth. Her ordeal on Friday had left her nervous about being alone in a deserted corridor, and for good reason.

Except she was being ridiculous. There were plenty

of other people in the building. The security guard, Tim, was within shouting distance.

A thump sounded, and she froze. Cocking her head, she strained to hear over the raindrops pummeling the roof. Her imagination was getting the better of her.

She forced herself to put one foot in front of the other, careful to avoid the stacks of tools and construction equipment piled near the floorboards. No wonder this area was supposed to be off-limits to patients. Still, she was thankful the nurse had made an exception. She wasn't ready to face the possibility of running into someone she knew but didn't recognize just yet.

The break room was compact with a row of vending machines on one side, and a sink, refrigerator and single cup coffee maker on the other. The glare from the freshly waxed floor was almost painful.

"See Emma?" she said aloud to bolster herself. "Nothing bad could happen in a room this clean."

Two tables, each set with four bright orange molded chairs, were scattered throughout the space.

Determined to get ahold of herself, she turned toward the coffee maker. A variety of single-serve cups overflowed the basket, and she chose one labeled Breakfast Blend. Fisting her hand around the plastic, she squeezed her eyes shut, welcoming the pain as the sharp edges dug into her palm.

This wasn't fair. Why did she instinctively reach for the coffee she liked, but she couldn't remember her own name?

Emma. Emma Lyons.

She snorted softly. Her name could have been Jane Doe for all the sense "Emma" made to her.

As she reached for the coffee maker, the room plunged into darkness. Blood rushed in her ears. She took a cautious step toward the exit, her hands outstretched like a blind, lurching mummy. Gooseflesh pebbled her skin.

Someone was in the room with her. She didn't know how she knew; she just did.

"Hello?" she called, her heart hammering against her ribs. "Tim?"

Fabric dropped over her head and strong arms crushed her middle, robbing the air from her lungs.

She expanded her chest to scream, catching a mouthful of cloth and the unmistakable odor of bleach.

A hand clamped over her face, and she clawed at the arm circling her waist. The man was taller than her and stronger. Her fingers sank into the soft flesh of his arm. He jerked her against his chest, and her injured shoulder throbbed in agony. Her vision blurred.

Her attacker squeezed tighter, and her knees grew weak.

"Don't faint on me," a low voice growled near her ear. "I'm not done with you yet."

Stars exploded at the edges of her vision, and she frantically stomped on the man's instep while simultaneously jabbing her elbow into his solar plexus. He grunted, his grip loosening. She struggled away but he yanked her backward, trapping both arms against her sides.

"You're a fighter," her attacker growled. "I like that."

Nausea threatened, and her rib cage ached. Her lungs felt as though they were going to explode. She lifted her foot to stomp again, but her attacker easily moved out of reach. The lack of oxygen was draining her. She had to breathe. Her muscles were weak and sluggish, refusing to cooperate.

An odd sense of calm invaded her chaotic thoughts. She was suffocating mere feet from safety. She couldn't give up. Not yet. Not now.

Her pulse thrummed, and with a burst of fury, she

wrested one arm free. Instinct took over. His eyes were vulnerable. She reached behind and above her, searching for his face, but the angle was too awkward. Tearing at the cloth instead, she managed to free her mouth.

As she let loose an earsplitting scream, a savage blow knocked her to the ground, and her attacker's low whisper vibrated near her ear. "We aren't finished yet."

THREE

Liam stuffed his phone into his pocket and glared at the slumbering security guard. No wonder his calls had gone unanswered. A paper cup with the last dredges of coffee rested on the floor beside the chair leg. The caffeine wasn't working.

He nudged the guard's toe with his foot. "Wake up, sunshine."

Tim slumped to one side. Liam's pulse spiked, and he lunged. He lowered the bulky guard to the patterned tile floor. Pressing two fingers to the base of Tim's throat, he noted a strong, steady pulse thumping beneath his fingertips.

The guard mumbled something, his eyes fluttering.

Liam glanced at the coffee cup. Had the guard been drugged? He showed all the classic signs of an overdose. Thankfully, the man's pulse was normal and his breathing steady.

Confident Tim was in no imminent danger, Liam straightened and shouldered his way into the patient's room. "Emma?"

The space was empty. The bed was neatly made. Forcing his emotions aside, he ran through the possible scenarios. There were no signs of a struggle. Though the hospital wasn't exactly teeming with activity, it also wasn't so deserted that someone could drug and kidnap

Emma without being noticed. She must have been forced out with a threat. But how long ago?

A sound brought him around so quickly his shoes squeaked.

"What's wrong with Tim?" A redheaded nurse in navy scrubs decorated with pink, frolicking kittens appeared. "What happened?"

She knelt before the prone man and began taking his vitals.

"I think he's been drugged," Liam said. "And don't touch that cup."

She gave a clipped nod. "I'll inform the doctor."

"Have you seen Emma? The patient in this room?"

"Went for coffee." The nurse jerked a thumb over her shoulder without taking her attention from the prone security guard. "Down the hall. Last door on the left."

A thump sounded. Liam glanced at the cordoned-off section of the hospital wing. Too early for construction workers.

Someone screamed, the sound cutting off abruptly.

A familiar rush of adrenaline surged through his blood. Retrieving his service weapon, he extended his arm. He crossed the distance and maneuvered through the plastic sheeting toward the sound.

"Emma!"

The corridor was plunged in darkness, and he reached for his flashlight before recalling he hadn't yet replaced the one he'd lost two days ago.

"Emma!" he called again.

His shin cracked against a stack of construction supplies. Righting himself, he fumbled for the wall, using his left hand to guide him through the pitch-black corridor.

His fingers bumped against a switch. The sudden shock of light temporarily blinded him.

A flash of orange sailed through the air, and a molded plastic chair bounced painfully off his forearm before clattering to the floor.

She came at him like a wildcat.

"Emma!" He stumbled backward, deflecting her blows, but not before she clocked him in the jaw. Stinging pain fired through his cheek. "It's me, Liam."

Recognition seemed to wash over Emma, and she sagged.

He quickly stowed his weapon with one hand and caught her against his chest with the other. "It's all right, it's over. You're safe."

"A man. There was a man." She turned her face into his shirt, muffling her voice. "He tried to suffocate me. He said…he said, *we aren't finished yet.*"

Liam's training urged him to follow the perpetrator, but his arms tightened around Emma. Catching himself, he pulled away. There were only two ways to exit the building from this location, and Liam had come from one of them.

"It's going to be all right." He threaded his fingers through her dark silken hair and urged her to meet his gaze. "Wait here."

The tips of her eyelashes sparkled with unshed tears, and his heartbeat tripped. Eyes like that were the reason cops quit hanging out with the guys after work and went straight home instead. They were the reason the pictures on their phones changed from deer camps to hospital nurseries. Eyes like that were dangerous.

"I'll be fine." She touched the bandage at her temple, her fingers trembling. "Catch him."

His senses vibrating on high alert, Liam sprinted the distance and kicked open the exit door to an empty parking lot on the far side of the building.

Sheeting rain hindered visibility. Forcing his fisted

hands to relax, he scanned the perimeter. No cars. No people. Nothing.

Traffic rumbled past on the highway to his left. A vehicle needed thirty seconds to melt into oblivion. At least three minutes had passed since he'd first heard the commotion.

Above his head, a shiny new security camera perched beneath the eaves. A wide grin spread across his face. Nothing like modern technology to make the job a little easier.

He rang the station for backup before returning inside.

The break room was empty, and he had a brief moment of panic before discovering Emma hovering outside her hospital room. Organized chaos reigned as orderlies along with Dr. Javadi wrestled Tim onto a gurney. The red-headed nurse, her hands encased in blue surgical gloves, handed Liam a plastic bag containing the empty paper cup.

"I didn't let anyone touch this," she said with a mournful glance at the prone security guard. "Like you asked."

He'd seen the nurse and the guard speaking earlier and sensed their relationship was more than casual.

Liam accepted the bag. "The break room is off-limits until further notice. It'll be taped."

"I'll let the staff know."

Dr. Javadi glanced up. "He should be all right. He's got a strong pulse and his airway is clear. Judging by the symptoms, I'm guessing he ingested an overdose of a prescription sleeping pill. I'll know more when the tox screens come back."

Liam had seen more than his fair share of overdoses. He didn't envy the guard the stomach pumping he was about to receive. "Keep me informed of his condition."

As the group rushed off, Liam touched Emma's elbow. "We should have someone check you out too."

"It's all right. I'm fine. Tim needs the help more." She pressed a fist to her mouth. "I thought he dozed off. I just left him there. I walked right past him."

"That's nothing. I nudged him with my foot and called him sunshine."

Her full lips formed a perfect O before she mumbled, "Yikes."

"That's putting it mildly." Not exactly his finest hour. At least Tim was young and healthy. Liam had no doubt he'd make a full recovery. "We can both apologize in person."

Her face was pale and devoid of makeup, making her appear younger than her age. She wore jeans with a wispy navy cardigan crossed double over her stomach, her white-knuckled fingers clutching the edges together.

He gently maneuvered her to a chair beside the bed. "Sit. Can I get you a drink of water?"

He'd give her a few minutes to collect herself—but not too long. He needed her observations of the attack while the memories were fresh. Keeping his rage at bay was secondary. He'd been filled with a nearly uncontrollable fury since discovering her empty room. Someone had done this on his watch. *On his turf.*

"I'm thirsty," she said. "But is it safe to drink anything?"

"Brought this from home." He retrieved a bottle of water from his pocket and twisted the cap. "About as safe as it gets."

She gratefully accepted the offering and wrapped her hands around the plastic.

"Are you certain you're not hurt?" he asked gently. "Adrenaline often masks injuries."

The first thing he'd felt after being shot was relief instead of pain. Relief that he was still alive. He'd known the bullet was coming the minute Swerve confronted him. Jenny's shouted accusations of his betrayal, and his subsequent denial that he was a cop, had only delayed the inevitable.

Swerve had been too distraught over killing Jenny to realize his intended target had survived. Sirens had followed. Maybe Swerve had called the ambulance in the hopes of saving Jenny, or maybe someone else had. Liam supposed it didn't mattered.

Emma swiped the back of her hand over her eyes. "He didn't hurt me. He caught me by surprise, that was all."

A violent shudder traveled the length of her body, and a wave of helpless frustration crashed over him. Maintaining a healthy distance with crime victims was part of the job. The only way to stay sane. Bad things happened to good people all the time. Jenny's death had shaken him, but he'd done what he'd always done—he'd boxed his emotions and tucked them away. He'd left the ultimate judgment to God. Emma's situation was dredging up feelings he thought he'd buried.

She needed a protector, and he'd already failed her once. Any distraction risked dangerous consequences for them both.

Her face averted, Emma tucked her dark hair behind one car, exposing the purple bruising on her temple from the car accident.

A wave of dizziness hit him hard, sweeping him into the past again. Swerve had backhanded Jenny the day before the shooting, and Liam had defended her. The response was instinctive. And fatal. His actions had triggered Swerve's suspicions, bringing into focus other incidents that might have escaped scrutiny while highlighting Liam's lengthy absence from the neighborhood after grade school. That was the risk of undercover work. There was never a way to escape inside a role completely. He'd tried to protect Jenny, and he'd gotten her killed instead.

With an effort born from years of practice, he shoved his personal feelings down. He knew better than anyone what happened when professional duties mixed with high emotions.

Nothing good.

He dragged a chair around to face Emma and sat. Leaning forward, he propped his elbows on his knees and intertwined his fingers. "I need to know exactly what happened. Tell me everything you remember. Every detail, no matter how small or insignificant it might seem."

She rested her hand over his, as though clinging to a lifeline. Despite his rigorous self-talk, he couldn't bring himself to pull away.

"Try and relax," he said. "Close your eyes if you need to. Tell me everything you remember.

Her throat worked. She appeared lost in the memory of what had just happened, and he doubted she even realized she was touching him.

She took another deep, shuddering breath. "I'm ready."

Gazing into the distance, she related the story with clinical precision to detail. She was a writer, he'd done his homework over the weekend, and her skills showed in her meticulous observations.

He'd spent the previous day researching her background. She was an investigative journalist who'd written a couple of novels. A sense of familiarity had nagged him, but he'd yet to discover why. Maybe she seemed familiar because she wrote about famous serial killers. According to her website, one of her books had been optioned for a movie.

The bottle of water in her hand crackled in her tight grip. "When I heard your footsteps, I thought he'd come back."

Liam jutted his sore chin. "You've got a mean right hook."

As though noticing her hand clutching his for the first time, she snatched her arm away. "I'm sorry. I couldn't let him catch me by surprise again. I don't know what happened."

"You were acting on instinct." He absently rubbed his thumb over the lingering warmth of her touch. "That's good. That's what's supposed to happen. You're tough. Sounds like you've had some self-defense training. Your body remembered what to do even though your mind may have forgotten the details."

She splayed her fingers and flexed them a few times. Her nails were neatly manicured ovals painted a dusky shade of pink.

She smiled tremulously. "I don't feel very tough."

"I've got the bruises to prove it," he joked, drawing delicate color to her pale cheeks.

Her gaze dropped, and she gasped. "You're hurt! You're bleeding."

He stretched out his leg. The second blow to his shin had opened the previous wound. The bleeding wasn't bad, just enough to soak through the material. The damage had already dried and darkened.

"It's nothing," he said.

She leaned forward, her hands outstretched. "I should take a look."

"No," he all but shouted, wincing as his voice echoed off the high ceilings. Exposing his leg felt too intimate. Too personal. He tucked his foot beneath the chair. "It's fine. Let's get back to what happened."

Despite the odds, she hadn't given up. She'd been ready

to fight with someone who was considerably bigger and stronger, and he admired her bravery.

Emma stood and moved a distance away, her arms wrapped protectively around her body. As much as he regretted the continued interrogation, the time immediately following the incident was vital. They both needed a little distance, and telling her story was the best way to achieve some perspective.

"Anything else you remember?" he asked.

"Like I said, I didn't get a good look at him. He was taller than me, but not by a lot. Maybe five foot eight or five-nine. Not an athlete. I jabbed him in the stomach." She absently rubbed her elbow. "I didn't hit a six-pack. I don't even know if I can identify his speech because he only whispered. That's all I can say."

A rumble of footsteps sounded in the corridor along with familiar voices. Bishop had arrived with the sheriff, easing the tension in Liam's shoulders.

Sheriff Bill Garner was the one saving grace that came from working in Redbird. With a solid history in law enforcement, the sheriff's experience showed. He'd already served twenty years in the Fort Worth Police Department when he ran for county sheriff. That was ten years ago. Now he was ten years away from pulling two pensions along with his social security.

Garner wasn't coasting toward his retirement, either. He worked hard, and he made sure Bishop and Liam did the same. All in all, he made life in Redbird infinitely more palatable. If he had a penchant for assigning nicknames that were more mocking than endearing, and if he occasionally had a sharp edge in his voice, most folks gave him a pass.

The sheriff spotted Emma and moved into the room. His gaze intense, he clasped one of her hands between both of his and leaned forward. "So you're the little lady that's been causing all the trouble."

"This is Emma Lyons," Liam said. "Emma, this is Sheriff Garner."

"You don't remember me, do you?" the sheriff asked, a bemused expression on his face.

Her brows knitted, and she shook her head.

"Probably for the best." The sheriff chuckled. "Gave you a speeding ticket about a week ago."

"Oh, uh, I don't remember," she mumbled.

The sheriff was showing his age with graying hair and a salt and-pepper goatee along with a barely noticeable paunch, but no one could fault his endurance or mental prowess.

"I wish I was here about something as simple as a traffic citation, Ms. Lyons," the sheriff said. "Do you mind if I steal my deputy for a moment? We're gonna let the doc check you out."

"I don't need a doctor," she said, her pose challenging. "I need to find out who wants me dead. I don't know if it's a boyfriend or some random crazy guy. Do you have any idea how that feels?"

Liam arched a brow. He'd yet to see this side of Emma—and he liked the juxtaposition. She was vulnerable, but she was no pushover. The sheriff needed to be challenged once in a while. They all did.

Garner sighed, his hands worrying the change in his pocket. "I'm real sorry, Ms. Lyons. We're doing everything we can."

Bishop knocked on the door frame to catch their attention, his expression grim. "We've got a problem. The security cameras in the parts of the hospital under renovation aren't wired yet. We've got no footage."

Liam's stomach curdled. "I was counting on that footage."

"Don't blame yourself," the sheriff said. "This close to the highway, he was long gone by the time you gave chase. We'll check the cameras on the other buildings in the area. Maybe they caught something. Looks like we've got someone familiar with breaking the law. Ms. Lyons is safe. That's what's important. You did good."

The sheriff's vote of confidence fell flat for Liam. He'd been marking time on the job. With only nuisance calls and drunk drivers to fill his days, his skills had slipped. Not anymore. The sheriff dealt with the same mundane problems, and he stayed sharp. The fault rested with Liam. He'd been a good cop in Dallas.

Redbird, for all its eccentricities, deserved a good cop, as well.

Emma toyed with her bangs, brushing them from her forehead. "What exactly does that mean? Why do you think the person who ran me off the road is familiar with breaking the law?"

"This isn't someone acting in a fit of rage," the sheriff explained. "This is someone who plans carefully. Methodically. Despite what you read in books, that's not something we see too often. Most crimes are impulsive, which means people make mistakes. We've got our work cut out for us."

Despite what you read in books… True crime.

The nagging voice in the back of Liam's mind surfaced with a howl. He'd previously discounted the connection as too far-fetched. In the absence of any other information, he had to reconsider the possibility.

He reached for his phone. "I know where to start looking."

"Now that's a loaded statement," the sheriff declared. "Care to elaborate?"

Liam scrolled through the glowing screen on his phone and flashed the picture that had sparked his initial suspicions. "She writes about serial killers. Someone with *methodical* patience wants to kill her. Doesn't take a lot to connect the dots."

Pressing her fingers against the tick-tick-tick banging in her head, Emma stared at the photo on the deputy's phone. "Are you certain I write about serial killers?"

She desperately wanted to remember, but even the idea left her queasy. None of this made any sense. What sort of person immersed herself in the mind of a killer?

Sheriff Garner squinted at the tiny screen. "I don't have my glasses. You'll have to explain what I'm seeing."

The sheriff's nose was prominent below deep-set eyes and he had a charming Texas twang. Deep creases formed parentheses around a mouth that seemed to naturally relax into an easy grin. Though he gave the appearance of being laid-back, Emma doubted many people crossed him. She sensed he ruled with an iron fist in a velvet glove.

Deputy Bishop guffawed. "It's a book cover. What does a book cover have to do with anything?"

Emma shivered and rubbed her upper arms. When the surly deputy had delivered her personal belongings, his attitude had been borderline rude. There was an expectant look on his face—a challenge in his questions. The encounter had left her with a feeling of unease she hadn't been able to shake. He didn't look well, either. There were dark circles beneath his eyes, and his skin was sallow.

"You're a true-crime writer. An investigative journalist with an impressive list of books to your name," Liam said.

He scrolled through the pictures and revealed a glossy publicity photo of her smiling face.

Gazing in wonder at the screen, she managed a be-mused, "That's me?"

She recognized herself from the face she saw in the mirror, though she didn't recall posing for the picture.

"Your last book was a number one bestseller," Liam said. "And, according to your website, optioned into a movie."

"At least I'm a successful writer," she said. "That's something, I guess."

"Last year, you bought a house in Redbird," he continued. "You moved here from Dallas. I thought I recognized you that first night, but I wasn't sure. I finally remembered. You wrote a series of articles for the *Dallas Morning News* about the Killing Fields. I must have recognized you from your picture in the paper."

The Killing Fields. She should probably know what he was talking about, but the name meant nothing to her.

Annoyance tightened her lips. She was heartily sick of playing catch up with her own life. "What are the Killing Fields?"

"A stretch of Interstate 45 between Galveston and Houston," Liam patiently explained. "It's known as the Highway to…well, let's just say it's the preferred dumping ground for serial killers."

A break in the clouds drew her gaze toward the window. Streaks of morning sunlight glittered over the rain-dampened trees. There was so much beauty in the world, why had she chosen to immerse herself in darkness?

"That sounds gruesome." She shuddered. "Why was I writing about the Killing Fields?"

"Twelve of the thirty bodies discovered on that stretch of highway in the past fifty or so years have been attributed to two different killers." Liam glanced up from his phone. "But eighteen of those victims remain open cases. All women."

The knots in her stomach pulled tighter. "Eighteen? That's…that's insane." She searched the faces of the three men for a mirror of her shock, but no one else seemed particularly outraged by the number. "Doesn't that seem like a lot?"

"We do what we can," the sheriff said with a hard, forced smile. "But one out of every three murders remain unsolved."

"History tells us that serial killers don't stop until they're caught," Liam added. "If our suspicions are correct, then he's still out there."

Nausea welled in the back of her throat. *He's still out there*.

There was a chance that someone who'd killed before without mercy wanted her dead, and he'd nearly succeeded.

Twice.

FOUR

"Wait a second." Bishop's close-set eyes narrowed. "You're saying she brought a serial killer to Redbird? That's a stretch, don't you think?"

Emma started. A memory flashed in the deep recesses of her thoughts, just out of view, like a moth beating its wings outside a window.

"Easy there, Bishop." The sheriff placed a hand on the deputy's gaunt shoulder. "We don't want anyone overhearing our little chat and starting a panic. We're only speculating."

A sense of urgency swirled through Emma's head like billows of smoke. Chasing down the memories was like navigating through a dense fog.

Deputy Bishop bounced his fist against his knee. "Don't those guys usually leave a calling card or something? This is a waste of time. I'm following up on the jealous boyfriend angle. Ninety-nine times out of a hundred, it's the significant other. Probably he's been threatening her for years."

"Then why isn't there a single report of a domestic altercation under her name in the police records?" Liam challenged.

"Maybe she's been protecting him. Happens all the time, and you know it."

Emma's throat closed. The tick-tick-tick in her head grew louder. There was something just out of reach. She felt it. Helpless frustration curled her hands into fists. Her body was letting her down. Her mind was letting them *all* down.

The sheriff was staring at her as though she might volunteer an answer, and she shook her head. "I honestly don't know if I have a boyfriend—jealous or otherwise. None of this sounds familiar."

"Too bad your phone is waterlogged," the sheriff said over a tired sigh. "We could at least contact the most-used phone numbers."

"Assuming she remembers the code," Bishop added with a smirk.

He didn't believe she had amnesia. Sure, her story sounded far-fetched—even to her own ears—but the sheriff and Deputy McCourt believed her.

Or maybe they were simply better at hiding their doubts.

"We can't afford to ignore the possibility of a connection to one of her books," Liam said, his callused finger tapping against the phone screen. "You specialize in Texas serial killers."

Pictures flashed in her mind like slides across a screen. Faces. People she didn't recognize though their features swam before her, taunting her. When she reached for the memories, they slipped further out of reach.

Disgust welled in her chest. Why couldn't she remember?

"I don't get the connection." The sheriff tilted back his head and stared thoughtfully at the ceiling. "All those cases have been solved. Doesn't make any sense. There's no motive."

"What about the Killing Fields murders?" Liam asked. "Eighteen additional bodies. That's a lot of unsolved crimes. Maybe she stumbled onto something and worried someone."

Her ears buzzed. All those women murdered and abandoned. Their deaths unsolved. What must that be like for their loved ones? For their families?

Hopelessly desperate, she appealed to Liam. "You read the articles. Did I name a suspect that might want to silence me?"

"Yeah, McCourt," Bishop said, his nasal voice grating on her nerves. "You did your *homework*, right? What else can you tell us about her?"

Emma shrank from the deputy's pointed appraisal. He was studying her more than helping her. As though he was cataloging her reactions and searching for inconsistencies.

The sheriff glared at him. "Stand down, Bishop."

"She named the Lonestar State Killer," Liam said. "No surprise there. He was never caught. People have suspected everyone from politicians to famous touring musicians. Nothing has ever come of it, though. Most people think he's dead. There hasn't been a new victim in over a decade."

"He hasn't killed recently that we know of," the sheriff corrected. "You said it yourself. Serial killers don't stop until they're caught. They want the attention. What's the point of committing a crime if they don't get the credit? If they don't get the fame? He's either dead or he's moved to another jurisdiction."

Their voices echoed around her head, and she tuned out their conversation. They were including her and ignoring her at the same time—which was a disquieting feeling.

She had to consider the facts impassively, without judgment.

She had temporal lobe swelling, but the doctor had hinted there was more memory loss than accounted for by the damage. He'd said that the brain had a way of protecting itself from trauma. For some reason her mind had chosen to become a stranger to her.

Had she erased something important? If so—why? Was she protecting herself—or someone else?

Liam gestured with his phone, jolting her back to the present. "What if it's a relative of a killer or a copycat? Someone connected to one of the subjects? Someone who didn't like how they were depicted in one of Emma's books?"

"It's a solid theory," the sheriff said. "Contact her publisher. See if she's gotten any death threats lately. We can't rule out anything yet."

Anxiety leached the air from her lungs. The same frustrating questions bobbed to the surface. They were all shooting in the dark. What had she chosen to forget? Why had she chosen to forget? She was trapped in this nightmare with no way of knowing who wanted her dead.

Liam cast her a sharp glance, and she kept her face impassive. He was far too sensitive to her moods.

The sheriff jabbed a stubby finger at Liam's phone. "What's she working on now?"

"Doesn't say." Liam studied the screen. "Only says the book will be released next year. I can do some digging on that too. Maybe she's writing about an unsolved case, and research on the new book stirred up a hornet's nest."

Emma huffed. That was putting it mildly. She tapped her heel in a rapid tattoo against the floor. People left traces of themselves behind all the time. She was more than a waterlogged phone and a totaled car.

What was more frightening? What lay before her, or what lay behind her?

"I need to see where I live."

At her sudden declaration, the three men turned abruptly to stare at her.

"I need to look for notes," she continued, a thread of steel in her words. "A computer. Anything."

"You will." The sheriff winked. "We just gotta wait until the doc says it's okay for you to leave. He's the boss."

"No. I'm the boss," she said through gritted teeth. "This is my life on the line."

Liam turned the screen toward her. "I understand your frustration. There's a lot we can learn about you without leaving the hospital. This is your latest release. See if that rings a bell."

His silvery blue eyes were filled with sympathy, and she focused her attention on the picture. Why was she lashing out? He was only trying to help. The accident had left her emotions raw.

She pressed her fingers against her brow bones and willed the memories to return.

The book cover featured a black-and-white portrait of an overweight, balding man with a thick neck and dead eyes. The title was written in bloodred, melting script: *Killer Instincts*.

Her head throbbed, and the room dissolved. Her breathing grew shallow.

The three men in the room faded away, leaving Emma a mental vision of a grisly double homicide in vivid detail.

Panic clawed through her. The horrific details scorched her brain, and she rubbed her eyes until she saw stars, willing the image away.

If this was her past, she no longer wanted to remember.

Liam knelt beside her. "What is it? Did you remember something?"

"No. Yes. An image." Just as quickly as it had appeared, the vision melted away. "It's gone. It was a crime scene. There were two people who'd been shot. It was Christmas. There was a tree in the corner of the room. Lots of presents." She was rambling. Capturing the details to give herself a sense of distance. "The dead man was wearing a blue flannel shirt. The woman was..."

The image of the woman was too horrible to repeat. Emma's vision grayed around the edges, and the room seemed to tilt.

"Breathe," Liam ordered gently, his calm voice centering her. "Think of something else. Replace the images with something good."

She flashed to him leaning over her, the rain streaming from his dark hair, and an immediate sense of peace enveloped her. Liam had saved her. She was grateful. But to him she was simply another problem to solve. Another case added to the staggering workload that had worry lines flaring from the corners of his eyes.

She physically shook her head, clearing the memory, and thought of the rust-colored dog instead. The Duchess was a good substitute. *Almost.*

"That's all I remember," she said. "At first, I was there, but then I was able to separate myself from the images. It was more like I was looking at a picture."

In that brief instant, everything had seemed vivid and real, and her emotions had responded in kind. She'd placed herself at the scene, but when she'd looked closer, she'd realized she was on the outside staring in. She obviously had a graphic imagination. An asset for a writer, no doubt.

"You didn't remember anything more personal?" Liam asked. "A detail from your life?"

"No. Nothing."

Her stomach lurched. After battling to remember, why hadn't she summoned a memorable vacation or her first pet? Why not think of a friend or a relative—her brother, at least?

Her mind was like a row of empty picture frames. A

cold gathering of backgrounds with no sentiment and no recognizable faces, as though someone had stripped away her past, leaving only blank canvasses.

"Hmm." The sheriff rubbed the back of his neck. "A couple killed around Christmastime. Ring any bells, Mc-Court?"

"No." Liam moved away, and the air around her seemed to chill without his comforting presence. "But it shouldn't take too long to sort through the serial killers she profiled."

The images crept back, and she focused on Liam, forcing them away. The deputy's hair was shaggy and his beard a little too long. There was no one taking care of him. No one to tweak his sideburns and remind him he needed a haircut. No one to keep him from working too hard. He'd kept watch over her until Tim had arrived that first night, and the stack of paperwork he'd retrieved from his SUV had towered on the floor near his chair.

The fatigue, the tiny imperfections in his looks, only added to his appeal, and she wrestled against an instinctive urge to care for him. To smooth the creases from his forehead. A troubled undercurrent flowed beneath his calm demeanor. There was something worrying Deputy McCourt, something that kept him up at night beyond his work schedule.

He caught her eye, and her heart did a little hopscotch. She was drawn to him. Was her response to him real, or was she merely clinging to the only familiar face in her shattered memory?

Liam retrieved a memo pad from his uniform pocket along with a pen. "You were probably recalling a photo from one of the crime scenes you researched. I'll look into it. Write down everything you remember before any time passes. We'll see what we can discover."

Once she accepted the paper and pen, he rested his hand on her shoulder and a calming warmth spread through her limbs. How did he manage to do that? How did he know just the thing she needed when he barely knew her?

When she didn't even know herself.

The hollow ache in her heart expanded. She was frantic to push this miserable loneliness aside. For one desperate moment she wanted to grasp his hand and press her cheek into his palm. She longed for a connection to someone, and he seemed to appreciate how lost and confused she felt.

Fearful of revealing her feelings, especially with the other two men hovering near, she bent her head and scribbled as many details as she recalled. She was no better than a drowning person clawing for help. Her weakness wasn't doing any of them any good. She was vulnerable and not hiding her fear very well. Better to keep a tight grip on her feelings until she knew more about herself.

If he needed details, it was the least she could do to help him.

Data scrolled through her head like information across a computer screen, and she swallowed around the lump in her throat. The couple had been celebrating their first Christmas together. When they failed to arrive at a family dinner, the woman's brother had volunteered to check on them. Haunted by what he'd discovered, years later he'd driven his car into a tree. His death was instant. His blood alcohol level was three times the legal limit. Though not directly, the killer had claimed another victim.

Horror mixed with excitement. "Dr. Javadi was right. Once I remembered the photo, I remembered more details surrounding the event. It's not much, but it's a puzzle piece."

"One of many, I expect," Liam said with an encouraging smile. "Be patient. If one thing has come back, then more will come back. That's easy for me to say, I know. But this is encouraging. One memory will lead to another and another and another."

Her past was taking jagged shape. This was her life. She recognized that. She interviewed murderers and their families. She searched for clues that other people missed. She craved understanding and healing for the victims. Murder had a way of collapsing in on itself like a black hole, sucking everything into its wake. Violent death was a community affair. No one close to the victim remained unscathed.

Everything that had seemed foreign to her moments before was suddenly clear. She gave the murder victims a voice. The dead were not simply names scrolling across the evening news, they were once living, breathing people with rich beautiful lives. She wasn't ghoulishly reliving the crimes. She wrote about the people who were lost, and the families they left behind. That was her legacy.

She glanced at Liam, wanting to explain, but unsure how. He didn't appear to judge her for her work, yet she'd judged herself.

The sheriff leaned forward and glanced at her notes. "That's good stuff. Can you build on that to fill in something from your personal life?"

She reached deeper before she felt it once more—the wall against her memories. A lock she couldn't open.

"No," she said, exhaling a pent-up breath. "Nothing." The moment she gave up on trying to remember, the tick-tick-tick in her head abated. "I'm still trying to wrap my mind around all this."

"Sometimes we do things for the greater good," Liam said, his gaze not quite meeting hers. "Things other people don't understand."

His expression remained shuttered, piquing her curiosity. What had Liam done for the greater good? She sensed the answer to what kept him up at night was buried in that question.

When he faced her once more, the implacable mask was back in place. "The articles you wrote for the *Dallas Morning News* were compelling. I must have recognized you from your bio, but it took me a while to put it together. You're the reason those women haven't been forgotten."

Bishop grunted. "Or maybe someone didn't like her making a living off of other people's misfortunes."

"It's not like that," she rasped, her own insecurities rushing back. "I write about people."

"Ease off, Bishop," Liam growled. "You know better than anyone that some crimes need the press to justify the man-hours. When victims are forgotten, their cases go unsolved. High visibility attracts more resources."

Emma's emotions hovered between relief and doubt. Bishop's words had sliced directly to the heart of her uncertainties. Was she truly keeping the women's memories alive, or merely capitalizing on tragedy? Would they be unforgotten without her?

Unforgotten.

The word sparked a flare of emotion. It meant something to her—but what?

She made a mental note to search for references in her personal belongings. There was something tenuous attached to that word—something that was just out of reach. She'd start with her computer and see if there was anything in her notes. Maybe she'd spark another memory to build on.

Sheriff Garner rested his elbows on a tall counter at his back and crossed his ankles. "Let's go back to what we know for certain. Can you tell us anything about the vehicle that forced you off the road? Make, model, even a number from the license plate?"

"No. Nothing. I want to tell you more." Searching for the details was causing a pounding headache. "A white truck. That's all I remember."

Someone outside this room wanted her dead. Someone wanted her memories erased with her forever.

Liam drifted to her side once more. "Maybe we should give it a rest for today."

Tears pricked at the edges of her eyes.

"I'm fine," she said with a false smile. She didn't need them treating her like a fragile, wilting flower even if she currently felt like one. "Don't worry about me."

She'd take some aspirin for her headache. There it was again. *Aspirin.* She knew about aspirin, but she didn't know who wanted her dead. The next book she wrote was going to be about the mysterious, frustrating effects of brain injuries.

"Well, shoot." Sheriff Garner chuckled, draining the tension from the fraught moment. "You're gonna give good ol' Redbird a bad name pretty soon. I wanna help, but I'm in kind of a pickle. First off, you can't hardly spit a watermelon seed around these parts without hitting a white pickup truck. Second off, I got no witnesses. Not many folks were out driving in that weather."

A knot of anxiety coiled in her stomach. "What are you saying?"

"My boys are good." Garner flipped his palms skyward. "The best. But we've got no security footage from this morning. We've got a break room full of fingerprints. Too many. Your guy didn't have the decency to leave us a calling card to identify himself. We'll keep investigating, don't you worry, but anything you can remember will help us."

"What if I can't remember?" She plucked at a loose thread securing a button to her navy cardigan. "What then?"

Her hand drifted to her throat. She hadn't imagined

the man's hands squeezing her—the breath trapped in her lungs. He'd been toying with her. He'd *wanted* to scare her. He'd enjoyed her fear.

A shiver snaked through her. When she thought about him, she felt as though she'd never be warm again.

The sheriff made a clicking sound with his tongue. "I'm going to put my best man on the case. Deputy McCourt is the lead investigator. If anyone can get to the bottom of this, it's him."

Deputy Bishop's head snapped up. "But—"

"No arguments." The sheriff flashed his palm. "I need you on the fraud investigation. Ms. Lyons will re-create her life with McCourt's help. I want to know everything there is to know. Start with where you went to kindergarten and don't stop until you know what you did last week." He replaced his Stetson. "Now for the bad news. The department doesn't have the time or the money for twenty-four-hour security. Tim is out of commission, but you've got McCourt for the rest of the day. I'll make some calls, see if I can shake some cash loose. Until then, stay vigilant. No more wandering off alone. I'm going to clear out and let you get some rest, ma'am." He touched the brim of his cowboy hat in a courtly gesture. "Liam here will take good care of you. I'm only a phone call away if you need anything."

"Thank you," she replied automatically.

In light of everything that had happened, his words were kind—though hollow. He was trying to warn her that catching her attacker was going to be nearly impossible even without the additional handicap of her amnesia.

She didn't need her memory intact to read between the lines.

Deputy Bishop sullenly trailed the sheriff from the room while Liam stayed behind, and the silence stretching between them grew heavy.

There was part of her that wanted to stay in the dark—to deny she wrote about killers for a living. Deny that she may have unleashed a monster. Her life was returning in odd snippets. She recalled all the details around the crime scene, but the rest of her life was blank. The only thing she knew for certain was that someone wanted her dead.

Liam braced his hands on the foot of the bed, leaning forward, his hair falling across his forehead. "The sheriff is right. Let's see what we can piece together about your life first. That should tell us something about your state of mind."

At the resignation in his voice, her heart sank. He was the only person she trusted, and he clearly wanted no part of the case. Even taking into account his obvious reluctance, she much preferred his company to Deputy Bishop's. At the very least, he was better looking.

She pressed her fingertips over a revealing smile. She didn't have to know who she was to know she found him attractive. He was even nice in a gruff sort of way. She obviously liked brusque, bearded men with silvery blue eyes.

Liam tilted his head, his expression awash with concern. "You all right?"

"Yes," she said, heat creeping up her neck. "Fine."

She silently chastised herself for the lapse. This wasn't the time for daydreaming. He was only doing his job. It was up to her to take charge of her forgotten life.

"I'm fine." She cleared her throat and dropped her hand. "Trying to digest everything that's happened."

"We don't need to start now. You need rest."

Her temper flared. There it was again. The assumption that she didn't know her own mind. She had a brain injury. She wasn't a child.

"I don't need to rest," she said through gritted teeth. "I need to find out who wants me dead."

Liam pressed the back of his hand to her forehead, and his small act of kindness was nearly her undoing.

"Are you sure you don't need a little time?" he asked. "You've been through a lot."

Unwelcome tears burned behind her eyes, and she nearly sobbed aloud. She was tired and hungry and unbearably alone. She was confused, and the adrenaline from her encounter was wearing off.

An overwhelming lethargy had taken its place. "I feel as though today started two weeks ago and won't end."

"That's normal," Liam said. "To be tired after an attack."

"I can't remember when I last ate," she mumbled. "I'm hungry."

"Then let's take care of that."

The way he said it, as though she was a child who'd forgotten to eat when actually she'd been assaulted and questioned for half the day, made something snap inside her.

"That's what I was trying to do!" she replied with a little too much attitude.

"Okay," he said, his expression devoid of censure.

A battle raged within her. She wanted to trust him, but something held her back. She appreciated his kindness, yet she was repaying him with hostility. What instinct from her forgotten past was urging caution?

She stilled, a question raging in the deep recesses of her brain. *What if she grew to count on him, and he let her down when she needed him most?*

The tick-tick-tick pounded in her skull, forcing her away from the question.

She had to concentrate on something within her power to control—things like getting something to eat. This introspection was getting her nowhere.

A covered meal, long since cooled, languished on the rolling tray beside her bed. It had been sitting there since she woke, but maybe there was something salvageable. Her stomach growled, and she reached for the stainless-steel dome.

Sucking in a breath, her fingers went slack. The lid clattered to the floor, the jarring sound echoing through the unnatural silence.

One moment the deputy was behind her, the next he was before her, his arms splayed protectively.

"What's wrong?" he demanded.

Her pulse racing, she pointed. "My attacker *did* leave a calling card."

A scattering of bullets, gold with copper tips, rested on the plate.

FIVE

Liam's phone buzzed and he jumped, then glanced around to see if anyone had noticed. He was on edge, his control inching away with each breach of security. There was no way to know how or when the bullets had been left.

This guy was toying with them while they flailed around in the dark like idiots.

Keeping Emma safe was his top priority, and judging by today's events, he was failing miserably. His darkening mood hadn't gone unnoticed, and he'd stepped outside to get his head straight. The anger was directed inward, and it was eating at him.

His phone buzzed again. He glanced at the number and groaned. It was his landlady. He'd left the dog in her care hours ago with assurances of a speedy return. So much for keeping his promises.

"Yes, Mrs. Slattery?" he answered, bracing for a rebuke.

After discovering the bullets, he'd called the county crime lab and they'd bagged and tagged the evidence. The sheriff was skeptical they'd find anything useful, but they had to go through the motions. The team was getting close to wrapping up, and a painfully young technician was loading the last of his equipment into the van.

"I've got dinner in the crockpot," Mrs. Slattery said. "It's a pot roast."

Because he'd been expecting annoyance, Liam's brain

took a moment to translate her words. A pot roast filling the house with a mouthwatering aroma sent his stomach growling. He couldn't recall the last time he'd eaten beyond a bite or two of sandwich sometime that afternoon.

He replayed Emma's earlier irritation when she was hungry and allowed himself a moment of amusement. Her annoyance hadn't bothered him; he'd recognized her frustration. Especially now, when he was starving himself.

He checked the technician's lingering progress. "You know I can't resist, but I probably won't be home until late."

"Another hour won't hurt a crockpot meal," Mrs. Slattery said. "Everything all right? I spoke with Bill at the mailbox. He heard there was a stabbing at the hospital this morning. I also talked with Rick at the meat market. He said there was a car accident and an amnesia case. I thought for certain he was lying, but Jessica at the checkout said she'd heard the same thing. Amnesia? Of all things. Does that actually happen in real life?"

"Not a stabbing. There was an…incident." The rumor mill in town never ceased to amaze Liam. Although he didn't mind as much when Mrs. Slattery was curious. She asked questions, but she never pressed him for answers. "I should be wrapping up soon. Sorry to leave the dog with you all day. I'll make it up to you. Didn't you say the upstairs sink was running slow? I'll clear the drain."

"After all you've done for me, I'm happy to do you a favor now and again," she said. "Oh! I almost forgot. About Duchess. I called the vet. He said he'd swing by when she delivered."

Liam held his phone away from his ear and stared at the screen. "Delivered what?"

"Puppies, I presume." Mrs. Slattery chuckled. "Why did you think she was waddling around with her stomach practically brushing the floor!"

"I thought she was fat." Liam hadn't been around animals much growing up, and he'd never had time for one as an adult. Still, Mrs. Slattery had a point. He'd been distracted as of late, but even *he* should have recognized the dog's condition. "So. Uh. Is there anything we should do for her?"

Puppies? That was out of his wheelhouse. Asking Mrs. Slattery to look after a dog for a few hours was far different from asking her to take care of a litter. What on earth was he going to do with a bunch of puppies if he couldn't find the owner? He didn't have the time or the resources to care for them. Sending the dog off to the shelter didn't feel right either. Not in her condition.

"Don't worry. She'll be fine." Mrs. Slattery's voice rose an octave in that way people did when they were trying to reassure someone without being patronizing. "Dogs seem to know what to do. She's made a bed in the dining room. It's better if she stays here. She'll be all alone at the shelter. I'm more worried about you. Are you sure you're all right? You sound tired. I don't think you've slept more than a few hours this whole weekend. You've got to take better care of yourself. You'll come down with something."

"We've been swamped around here," he said, rubbing a weary hand over his eyes. "And it's not letting up anytime soon."

"Is it the amnesia victim?" Mrs. Slattery trilled. "It's true then, isn't it? It's such a coincidence. I'm reading this book where the killer forgets he murdered his wife. I'm practically an expert on amnesia now."

"You're a worse gossip than the mailman." Liam chuckled. Despite her zealous curiosity, he trusted Mrs. Slattery to keep a secret. He had a professional responsibility, though, and nothing trumped duty. "You know I can't talk about my cases."

"I know." She huffed. "But you can at least let me use my imagination. Nothing ever happens in this town. Don't worry if you get home late. I'll be up past midnight reading *Deadly Memories* tonight."

Mrs. Slattery didn't know the half of it. "No promises. Eat without me."

"Take care of yourself. This might be a sleepy little town, but I worry about you."

The declaration startled him until he recalled that Mrs. Slattery had lost her only son in Afghanistan a decade before. Her grief over the loss was as fresh as if he'd died the day before. That probably accounted for her concern.

"You know me," Liam said. "I'm always careful."

"We're not immune out here, you know. There was that murder twenty or so years ago. Also they found the body of that girl in the next town over last year. Course, they don't think that was a murder. They think she overdosed, but still."

"It's a real crime spree."

He mostly kept Mrs. Slattery at arm's length, but she didn't make it easy. Sometimes he hoped the odd friendship they'd forged might last. But he knew better. He'd passed through enough homes during his childhood to realize she wouldn't miss him when he was gone. Out of sight was out of mind, which was probably for the best. When he returned to Dallas, he didn't want anything tethering him to the town. *No loose ends. No regrets.*

She'd find another boarder. Someone to fix the sink and rake the leaves. Someone who was home more often and was better company. Liam didn't have any illusions as to his worth. But when she fussed over him, he worried he was taking advantage of the situation.

"You know, Liam," she said. "You're always welcome to bring a guest for supper."

"Who?" he asked automatically.

"A girl, perhaps. You know, as in, a girl who is a *friend*."

He mentally slapped his forehead. He'd walked right into that one. She'd been trying to fix him up lately. He hadn't taken the hints right away, so she'd ramped up her efforts.

"You know I'm not seeing anyone," he said. And had no plans to change. As a kid, he'd watched movies about happy families like other kids watched fairy tales—they were fantasies that didn't happen in real life. "You know me."

"Which is your own fault. I could have three dates lined up for you with a snap of my fingers."

The sheriff stepped through the hospital exit, and Liam straightened away from his SUV. "I gotta go, Mrs. Slattery. I'll try and make it home by six."

"You sure you don't want me to snap my fingers?"

"Positive."

She kept sending him to the grocery store for the oddest items, and he had a sneaking suspicion she was trying to fix him up with one of the checkout workers. Not that there was anything wrong with the checkout workers; he simply wasn't looking for a relationship. Especially not now. One of these days she was bound to give up.

"I'll make sure there's a plate set out for you," Mrs. Slattery said. "No matter how late you are."

"Thanks."

He stowed his phone once more. Her quiet confidence only increased the pounding in his skull. If he missed another dinner, he'd be letting her down. He seemed to be letting everyone down these days. Maybe that's why she'd been trying to fix him up. He'd overstayed his welcome. If the case in Dallas didn't wrap up soon, he'd look for other accommodations.

"Sheriff!" he called. "Wait up."

"Whaddya need?" Garner's hand dropped from the handle of his truck and he stuck both of them in his pockets. "I gotta get something to eat before my stomach chews a hole all the way through to my backbone."

"I think we should call in the FBI on this one."

Liam hedged his bets against asking for the Texas Rangers. They'd take the case, but the FBI was less of a threat as long as the sheriff felt he had control of the situation.

"Huh." The sheriff rocked back on his heels. "The FBI? We don't need those boys tromping around our little town."

Liam was accustomed to working with the guys from the Organized Crime and Gang Unit. Law enforcement around here wasn't as comfortable sharing jurisdiction. They tended to circle the wagons when there was a problem.

"We're in over our heads," Liam said. The rain had finally stopped, leaving the parking lot island a trampled, muddy mess beneath the overcast sky. "We don't have the manpower to take on a case this size. There's a chance this guy has committed crimes across multiple jurisdictions. If he's acted before, they may already be trying to track him."

"Look, I know you like this girl." The sheriff rubbed his chin with a thumb and forefinger. "But what do we know about her?"

A flush of heat spread across Liam's face. "She's the victim of a crime. That's my only interest."

"A pretty victim." The sheriff winked. "I can't call in the FBI without more evidence. No one saw Ms. Lyons get run off the road. We've got no video proof that anyone was in the hospital. For all we know, she planted the bullets herself."

"Tim didn't drug himself," Liam said with a hardness

he didn't normally use with his superior. "And don't forget the paint on the car."

"We don't know how long that paint's been there. Ms. Lyons was prescribed sleeping pills the last two evenings. What if she didn't take them? What if she saved them up?"

Anger building inside him, Liam widened his stance. "I believe her."

His faith had nothing to do with his feelings for her—however confusing those might be. He was trusting his gut. There was no way she'd drugged Tim.

"I believe her too," the sheriff said. "I'm only telling you what they're going to tell me, I can't exactly call in the Feds with nothing but a bucket of circumstantial evidence." The older man seemed to read something in Liam's expression, and he shrugged. "All right. I'll see if I can call in a favor. Until then, stick to her like duct tape on a broken taillight. This thing isn't going to be easy. You're not gonna be happy about what I have to say."

Liam's nostrils flared. "Why?"

"I didn't want to tell you until I was absolutely certain. I know you like this girl, but she's wrapped up in something *real* bad. The Feds might come to us. This thing goes deep."

The sheriff had a few quaint euphemisms for common problems the deputies encountered. "Real bad" was code for drugs. Redbird was too far north for the worst of the violence, but no one in Texas ever remained unscathed.

Illegal substances poured across the border and hemorrhaged through the spiderweb of roads linking Texas to other lucrative markets.

Liam kept his expression impassive, hoping the sheriff didn't see the blood draining from his face. He felt as though someone was sucking the life out of him, depleting him.

"What did you find?" he asked, his voice deadly calm.

How had Emma gotten mixed up in something *real* bad?

The sheriff heaved a great sigh and closed one eye, his head tilted, as though he couldn't quite face Liam with the news full-on. "We got a preliminary DNA hit from a cigarette butt left on Emma's porch. Struck me as odd, you know. She doesn't smoke."

The M-Vac forensic DNA collection system stored DNA coding for easy searches and matching. The system had revolutionized law enforcement. Guys who'd committed atrocities twenty years before were popping up on the radar to finally answer for their crimes. In the old days, getting the DNA match had taken weeks. These days, it took only a matter of hours for a preliminary search.

Liam gritted his teeth and nodded. "Who?"

"Maximo Reynosa's first cousin, Juan Reynosa. He was picked up on a drug charge a couple years back. Made bail, then disappeared over the border again. That's how he got his DNA in the system."

Liam was afraid to look down for fear he'd see his hands were shaking. Reynosa was one of the most brutal cartel leaders in all of Mexico, and that was saying something.

"Okay," he said, his voice as smooth as polished glass, exuding a confidence he didn't feel. "If that's the problem, then we work the problem."

Keep it together. An itchy bead of sweat trickled down his neck. He was back in Dallas, standing before Swerve, denying he was a cop. The lie had come as naturally as a warm breeze on a spring day. The skill had served him well both then and now. He didn't want the sheriff seeing how rattled he was by the information. Not after that dig about his interest in Emma.

Liam didn't for a moment believe she'd gotten mixed up with Reynosa on purpose. Maybe she'd run across him while writing one of her articles. Maybe she'd written something Reynosa didn't like. Liam didn't suppose it mattered. The danger was here and now.

The sheriff jangled the change in his pocket. "You know what this means, don't you? There's a chance Reynosa is sending a message."

"Yep. I get the picture."

Liam recognized the same icy fear he'd felt staring down the barrel of Swerve's shaking pistol. There were some moments in a guy's life when he recognized that nothing was ever going to be the same.

If Maximo Reynosa was sending Emma a message, then she didn't have long to live.

The noises surrounding Emma were hushed and peaceful. Above her, a canopy of leaves spread dappled sunlight over a bed of pine needles. The air was warm, the breeze spring-scented. Voices from the campsite sounded in the distance along with the occasional burst of raucous laughter. Camping wasn't her favorite activity, but her new stepdad was an avid outdoorsman. Her mom wanted the two families to "bond." Whatever that meant.

Mom was determined that Emma and her new stepbrother get to know each other. Neither had been particularly interested. No one had asked Emma whether or not she wanted a new family, and yet she was expected to welcome these people into her life with open arms. Fat chance. She already had a dad, and he was dead. She didn't want a replacement. She wanted her real dad back.

Jordan snatched her hand. "C'mon," her new stepbrother urged. "Let's go to the lake. My dad says I can't go alone."

She yanked her arm away. "No."

"You're a chicken, aren't you? I bet you can't swim. I bet you're scared of the water."

A rare flash of insight caught her off guard. Jordan didn't want a sister any more than she wanted a brother. He was angry at the situation, something they had in common. She'd been too wrapped up in her own self-pity to realize he was suffering, too.

This was her chance to bridge the distance, to make things better between them. If she handed him an olive branch, he'd forget about the lake and turn back toward the campsite.

"I can swim better than you any day," she snapped.

"Prove it, Emma."

He took off first, gaining the head start. Together they ran, their bare feet flying over the dirt. He stopped suddenly, and she skidded into his back, pushing him forward. Her brief flash of empathy long forgotten, she elbowed her way around him. He'd cheated her for the win.

He stumbled and turned, his face pale. "We're going to be in so much trouble."

The scene changed, and she was standing in an empty ballroom. A figure appeared before her, his features blurred. He beckoned her to join him. As though pulled by an invisible string, she took a cautious step. She knew him. His name balanced on the tip of her tongue. There was no reason to be afraid.

She took another step. He lifted his arm and aimed a gun at her head. She opened her mouth to scream, but no sound came.

He pulled the trigger. In a flash of light, the bullet struck her in the head, propelling her backward. She was falling and falling, the windows above her collapsing inward. Shattered glass settled over her like a shroud.

She didn't feel pain, only betrayal. The man stood over her, and she managed to speak. "I trusted you."

Emma woke with a gasp, a fine sheen of perspiration coating her skin. Her heart boomed painfully in her chest. The dream was important. It meant something. There were details from her past imbedded in the images. She fumbled for her bedside phone and the card the deputy had left. He'd urged her to call him if she remembered anything, and she had to speak with him while the dream was fresh in her mind.

The line rang three times before a mumbled, "McCourt," sounded.

"I have a stepbrother," she blurted. "His name is... his name is... Jordan. My mom married his dad the year I turned ten. We went camping together one summer. Something happened. We got in trouble. I don't know what it was, but it was bad."

I bet you're scared...

Whatever happened that day had changed them both. *We're going to be in so much trouble.* The tick-tick-tick was trying to force her back, but this time she wasn't giving in.

"Jordan Harris," Liam said.

Searing pain splintered through her skull.

"What?" she managed to gasp.

"Your stepbrother's name is Jordan Harris. He works for—"

"The Department of Defense." A lava-spewing fissure cracked open in her brain, and an island of memories began to form. "I remember! He's always overseas. I think he's in China or something."

She and Jordan had stared daggers at each other across the aisle during their parents' wedding. Despite everyone's best efforts, nothing had bridged the distance. The camping trip had brought about a short-lived truce, but whatever they'd done that day had eventually driven them further apart. She was certain of it.

A thump sounded in her ear, as though Liam had dropped his phone.

"He works in the Middle East," the deputy said, his voice muffled and distant. "I've got some notes here. Iran or Iraq. The Department of Defense wasn't exactly forthcoming. They also said it could be a week or more before they can get a message to him. I'm sorry. I pushed. They know it's important. They're apologetic. It's classified. You get the picture. Whatever your brother does for the Department of Defense, it's not something they're willing to share."

Even when she finally remembered something, she was still playing catch up, and her temper flared.

She was heartily sick of everyone else having the jump on her. "Why didn't you tell me?"

"Sorry. I only just found out myself. Got a call from some lady at the Department of Defense right before bed. Thought I'd wait until morning before I briefed you."

She glanced at the clock and gasped. "It's 3:00 a.m.!"

"Yep."

"I'm so sorry." Her gaze darted around the darkened room. What was wrong with her? This impulsiveness felt out of character, but she wasn't certain of anything. Not anymore. "I, uh, I had a dream. I didn't realize what time it was. I shouldn't have bothered you."

"Don't worry about it. As long as I have you on the phone, I got a hold of your publisher. I can tell you everything tonight or I can wait until tomorrow."

Feeling only a brief stab of guilt, she said, "Why don't you give me the abbreviated version."

A few extra minutes awake wasn't going to hurt either of them at this point. Her past was returning, and she was anxious for more information. A bridge to whatever had set off this dangerous chain of events.

"No problem," Liam said. "Your next release is about the Lonestar State Killer. It's the first book you've written about a killer who's still at large, but you didn't name a suspect. You speculated the killer was former military. That's a pretty big pool of people. It's too vague to panic anyone."

Unforgotten.

The word was important.

There was something elusively familiar about his description of the book. A puzzle, though she wasn't quite certain of the picture she was trying to piece together. "All right. That's something."

"You haven't gotten any death threats. You did get a marriage proposal from some guy in Norway. He saw your picture on the back cover of a book and thought you'd be perfect for each other. He was insistent. That's when you hired a company to wipe your personal information, like family connections and addresses, from the internet. Most people don't realize how many layers deep you have to go to keep something as simple as your address from showing up on common search engines."

"Oh my."

"Don't worry. He turned out to be harmless." Papers rustled in the background. "Not to mention he's still in Norway. I checked. You and your editor don't talk much about your personal lives. She mentioned you'd gotten a lucrative contract on the movie rights to your bestseller. She thinks you might have some family money too. You don't have kids. We knew that. She said you joked about your lack of a dating life the last time you spoke. That was a week ago. Unless something crazy happened between now and then, I'm guessing you're not seeing anyone."

Relief shuddered through her. "That makes me feel

somewhat better, I suppose. I'd like to think that if I was dating someone, they'd be looking for me by now."

At least she didn't have to feel guilty about her unexpected attraction to the deputy. There was no boyfriend waiting in the wings when her memory returned completely. The spaces were filling in even though there were still enormous sinkholes she kept tripping into. At least the doctor had warned her this might happen.

"If they're not already, people are going to be very worried about you very soon, Emma," Liam said, lowering his voice and forcing her to press the phone closer to her ear. "Near as I can tell, no one was expecting to hear from you for several days. You were finishing up your book. There were a bunch of papers in your car, and you'd packed for an overnight somewhere. Your editor mentioned that you sometimes rent a hotel room right before a deadline for a marathon writing weekend. Which probably explains why no one has called in a welfare check yet. They're used to you going off the grid for periods of time."

She knew she had friends, though she couldn't explain why she was certain. The memories often started with a feeling before transforming into full-fledged recollections. Yet she couldn't shake a nagging sensation that she needed to get in touch with someone.

She'd reached for her phone a hundred times over the past few days only to find it gone, her muscle memory annoyingly intact. The habit assured her she was accustomed to keeping in contact with people.

"Okay." She'd started to think she was a crazy hermit with no friends. Turned out, she was actually a crazy hermit because of a deadline. That felt somewhat better. "Maybe it's a blessing that no one is worried yet. Maybe I'll have my memory back by the time they do."

A warm sliver of light showed beneath her door. The

sheriff was keeping watch tonight. Earlier she'd caught him balling up pieces of day-old newspaper and lobbing them into the trash bin.

She tilted her head for a better look. His shadow wasn't there, but she wasn't worried. Sometimes he walked the corridor to stretch his legs. He was only a few feet away, and yet that same gut instinct she'd felt after the car accident had urged her to call the deputy first.

Liam muttered something. "You mentioned a—" the word stretched around his obvious yawn "—dream. Did you remember something else?"

Her impressions were already fracturing and fading, and she grasped for the dissolving pictures. "Kind of."

The dream had started with a memory. The images were crisper and the feelings more like echoes. The second part, the man in the shadows, had felt different—hazy and unfocused. That portion of the dream had been symbolic. Not to mention they'd done enough tests to know if she'd been shot before. The shattered glass settling around her had felt like rain. Someone had betrayed her—but who? If only she'd been able to see the man's face.

Her head throbbed. *I trusted you.*

Trusting the wrong person had nearly gotten her killed. Her breath seized.

Without her memory, how did she know she wasn't making the same mistake again?

SIX

Emma stood, her gaze drawn to the window.

"You still there?" Liam nudged her back into awareness. "Everything okay?"

Had the figure been Jordan?

She didn't think so, but she wasn't certain. Jordan was real, that much she knew. Other feelings surrounded him, crowding together in a jumbled heap. As the past came rushing back, she felt as though she was drowning. While she craved the memories, they were materializing too fast, leaving her confused and disoriented.

She started to tell Liam about the dream, then stopped herself. Everything had seemed crystal clear before, but even rehearsing the words sounded ridiculous. She'd had a dream, and Liam still knew more about her life than she did.

"Everything's fine," she said, gripping the phone. She didn't need him rushing to the hospital at 3:00 a.m. because she was falling apart over a stupid dream. "The whole thing sounds dumb now that I'm saying the words out loud."

"Nothing is dumb. I'm not discounting anything. Even the smallest detail is significant."

"I'm pretty sure this is dumb."

"Look, if it helps, I was dreaming the Georgia Bulldogs were playing the Texas Longhorns in the Sugar Bowl. The teams were wearing the wrong uniforms. I kept yelling at the TV for everyone to change clothes. I don't see how your dream could be more ridiculous than that."

His confession earned a reluctant grin. "Okay. Here it goes. I was camping with my stepbrother. He challenged me, and I… I don't know how to explain it. I could have been nice to him, but I wasn't. We must have gotten into trouble, because in the dream, I knew if I hadn't been a jerk, everything would be different between us. I should have been nice to him, but I wasn't. There." She covered her guilt with a giddy burst of laughter. "Now you know the truth. I was a jerk as a kid."

"I hate to break it to you, but you're not special. All kids are jerks at some point or another."

Grateful they were speaking on the phone and not in person, she covered her burning eyes with one hand. The shame was familiar, as though she'd been carrying a heavy burden for a very, very long time. And yet, just like that, with one simple sentence, Liam had absolved her of the crushing guilt.

An enormous weight had been lifted from her shoulders.

She'd been a jerk. *Yes.* But Jordan hadn't been completely innocent, either.

"I suppose you're right," she conceded, another memory bubbling through the fissure. "Jordan used to parachute my Barbie dolls off the garage roof."

"See? Kids. That's what I'm talking about."

"You're very perceptive." She decided against telling him about the second part of the dream. There was nothing of substance to tell. "You must have had a brother or a sister growing up."

Liam coughed. "About your dream, do you think it has anything to do with what's happening now?"

Remorse stabbed at her resolve. So much for learning

a little about his personal life. The deputy was always kind and considerate, but more and more she realized there was a part of himself he kept hidden. A big part. She wanted to riddle him out the same way she wanted to puzzle out her memory.

"I don't think the dream is relevant," she conceded. The false excitement was wearing off, leaving her drained. She was annoyed with herself for waking him with something this inconsequential. "We were kids. It was a long time ago. I shouldn't have bothered you. It was just a dream. I don't know what I was thinking."

Great. He was probably regretting ever taking this case even more. She'd been in the hospital nearly three days, and she'd seen other patients come and go in that time. They'd all had visitors. Not her. She'd called Liam because she didn't have anyone else to call.

The island of memory forming around Jordan was merging into a continent, bringing a sense of overwhelming sorrow. Her stepbrother loved her, but they'd never gotten along well. Their parents had been their only connection, and when her mom passed away, that connection had frayed. Jordan's work was his life, and he wouldn't appreciate being called away from something important because of her.

That was a detail from her life she suddenly remembered vividly—Jordan's work was *always* important.

"He won't come," she said. "Don't bother."

"Who won't come?" Liam asked.

"Jordan won't come. We don't get along." The past rumbled over her like a freight train, leaving her emotions bruised and battered. Reliving her life was exhausting. "We argued the last time we spoke. It was about something stupid." Echoes of feelings reverberated through her chest. She'd never realized how closely memories and emotions were tied. "You can tell your contact at the Department of Defense not to bother tracking him down."

"Are you sure that's what you want? According to what we've been able to discover, he's your closest relative. You need someone looking after you."

You're doing that job just fine.

Once again, she was thankful he couldn't see her. She was coming to depend on him too much.

Even though Jordan could explain the dream, she wasn't going to risk Liam speaking to her stepbrother first. Not until she knew her role in the events that summer. Her feelings around the memory were muddled. There was fear but there was also shame. She wasn't ready for Liam to look at her the way Jordan had looked at her the last time they'd spoken.

"I'm sure," she said, forcing back a flood of grief. "Really. If he does get in contact, tell him it was a false alarm. He'll believe that."

A childhood memory was the least of her worries. She pictured a stack of boxes and recalled that she'd decided not to unpack her Christmas tree after the move. She was working on the book. Jordan was out of town. Her friends were back in Denver and busy with their own lives. She'd been busy too and had done a poor job of keeping in touch. There wasn't much point to a Christmas tree for a holiday spent alone. She'd called Jordan on Christmas Day, but he hadn't answered. She'd missed his return call.

They were both focused on their work, and friends and family were bound to suffer. That was months ago.

"Are you okay?" Liam asked quietly. "You sure you don't want me to come up there?"

"No, no. Of course not." She held the phone against her chest and sniffled, then took a deep breath before holding the receiver to her ear once more. This was precisely what she'd hoped to avoid. "Go back to sleep. I'm sorry I woke you."

"Don't worry about it. If you remember anything else, I'm here."

"Thanks."

"Listen to me, Emma," he said quickly, preventing her from hanging up. "You're not alone. You know that, don't you?"

The conversation between them was quiet and intimate, and her pulse drummed. He deserved a whole person, and her life was nothing but a heap of fractured memories.

"I know." She bit the inside of her lip. He was wrong; she was entirely alone, and her solitude was of her own making. "Don't worry about me. I'm fine. Really. The jigsaw puzzle is coming together, just like the doctor said."

Each piece connected to another. Huge gaps remained, but there were also moments of clarity. She was fascinated with serial killers. She investigated them for newspaper articles and wrote about them in her books.

The Lonestar State Killer had launched a black hole for her, and she'd fallen into the void. He was out there, and she had to find him. To stop him. Everything and everyone in her life had suffered because of it. She'd followed leads down the rabbit holes of internet message boards where amateur sleuths dealt in information sharing and backstabbing in equal measures. Everyone online was in a competition to find the killer, and trust was in short supply. The subterranean internet world was shrouded in shadows and operated apart from the regular channels of law enforcement.

"We're going to get through this," Liam insisted. "I won't quit until you're safe."

She snatched a tissue and smashed it against her nose.

There it was again. His uncanny ability to know what she needed, even when she didn't even know herself.

"Thanks," she squeaked over the lump in her throat and winced. "Sorry I woke you," she added, modulating her voice.

"No problem. Good night, Emma."

She hung up the phone and sat for a long moment. Tilting her head, she studied the light beneath the door. The sheriff's shadow hadn't returned. She crossed the distance and reached for the handle. Resistance met her efforts.

She yanked again. Nausea rose in the back of her throat, and she frantically rattled the handle. The edges of her vision blurred, and she scrambled for the phone once more.

She was alone. Someone had locked her in this room.

Footsteps approached, and Emma backed away, frantically searching for a weapon. She yanked the rolling table before her and braced her feet, her hands fisted before her.

A sharp staccato knock sounded, and the door swung open.

Deputy Bishop appeared, a frown puckering his brow. "Everything all right? I just took over from the sheriff, and I thought I heard voices."

"I'm fine." Trembling, she unfurled her hands and tucked her hair behind one ear. "Did you lock the door?"

"Come again?"

"The door." She clutched the table, keeping the flimsy barrier between them, just in case. "I tried to leave just now. The handle was locked."

"Not sure I follow. The door was open." He was thin and gaunt, his face an almost jaundiced shade of orange, his hair barely more than wispy wires atop his head. "How ya feeling? You remember anything more?"

He appeared genuinely bemused, and her pulse beat

erratically. The dream had rattled her, that was all. She was letting her imagination get the better of her. Maybe the door had simply been stuck. She was tired and not thinking straight.

"I've remembered some." She swallowed. Hard. "A little here and there, but nothing important."

She glanced around him into the corridor. The lights were dim, but she caught sight of the redheaded nurse crossing toward the duty station and heaved a sigh of relief. Even if he was a threat, there was nothing he could do to her. Not here. Not now.

"It'll come back," he said, circling the brim of his hat between his skeletal fingers. "Memory is a funny thing, isn't it? I forget things that happened this morning but remember things from my childhood clear as a bell. It's like we cling to the stuff that's been taking up space in our heads the longest."

Her knuckles had turned white where she clutched the table. "I never thought of it like that."

Maybe that's why her thoughts had drifted to her childhood. She was rebuilding her past from the base up. Her memories were coming back like connected rooms in a sprawling mansion. Each one led to another and another and another.

He scuffed his feet and stared at the patterned tile floor, then cleared his throat. "Ask McCourt to look into case file 1701. Might be something of interest there."

"Shouldn't you tell him?"

"No." The deputy replaced his hat in a gesture that told her he'd said all he had to say on the subject. "After everything that's happened, it's better that it comes from you."

He left, leaving her brittle and confused. His only crime was being a jerk. He didn't fit the mental image she had of her attacker. Closing her eyes, she recalled the feel of his hands around her neck. Bishop was too tall and slender. Or was he? Everything had happened so quickly that day, she didn't trust her memories.

She stared at the silver door handle, and her stomach dropped. Believing in God's charity didn't make her a fool.

Only one thing was certain. She no longer felt safe in this hospital, and she wasn't staying here another day.

"You're sure you're ready to leave?" Liam asked.

Standing beside her, he felt like the clumsy giant from his high school days, all elbows and knees and always taking up more space than everyone else. He'd grown too fast during those awkward years and hadn't always understood his own strength. He was forever knocking things over. Breaking things.

"I'm at a disadvantage no matter what," Emma said, appearing more fragile than the day before. "I could walk right past my attacker on the street and not even realize it."

"Exactly." Liam hadn't taken the danger seriously before. He wasn't making the same mistake twice. "Because of your memory loss, you're exposed outside of these four walls. At least think about staying here another night or two. The security cameras are all hooked up now. We'll be ready for him if he's stupid enough to try again."

He'd discovered no connection to Maximo Reynosa, but the cartel was careful to never leave a trail.

Not unless they wanted to.

What if the attacks were a warning? Something to do with Emma's work as an investigative journalist? A drug dealer operating around these parts made more sense than a serial killer. There were a couple of people in Redbird he had his eye on—people whose expensive cars didn't fit their lifestyles.

Liam made a mental note to run the hospital security

footage past Rose just in case. She'd lived in town the longest of anyone in the department. She'd spot someone who was out of place instantly.

Guilt flickered across Emma's delicate features, and she rubbed her forehead. "Here's the truth. I can't stay here any longer. I'm going stir-crazy. I feel trapped. Dr. Javadi said that reminder treatment was unreliable, but he didn't say it was worthless. I need to go home. I need to at least try. I need to find out if something familiar will jog my memory."

No one had seen or heard anything unusual the day of her disappearance. The department didn't have the manpower to keep watch over the empty house, which meant they were relying on the occasional drive-by of the property and observations from her neighbors. Not the most reliable surveillance, although Liam never underestimated the usefulness of a nosy neighbor.

"Is there anything else you're not telling me?" he asked.

"No, no. Of course not. Nothing."

Emma stared out the window, and he put himself in her shoes. As much as staying in the hospital kept the situation contained for law enforcement, they were no closer to discovering answers. She was gaining her memory in bits and pieces. If there was a chance something in her life might trigger a breakthrough, that was a chance worth taking.

"This guy wasn't scared off by a hospital full of people," she said. "Answer me this—what's the difference between sitting outside my room and sitting outside my house?"

"Not much," he grudgingly conceded.

He could easily install cameras at her house, as well. He happened to know they were in stock at the hardware store. He'd put in a set for Mrs. Slattery a month or two before.

"I rest my case." Emma stared out the window, her face

half in shadows, sunlight glinting off the honey-colored streaks in her chestnut hair. "Maybe it's better if someone else takes over my case."

"Hold on." He felt as though the air had been suctioned from the room. "Why do you say that?"

"Because you've been trying to shed the responsibility since Friday night, but it keeps falling back into your lap. Where does that leave us?"

The walls closed in around him. She was backing him into a corner. When they were dealing with a possible hit-and-run, Bishop was adequate for the job. The hospital attack had raised the stakes, but she obviously didn't have much faith in him. Why should she?

"I never said I didn't want the case." He clenched his back teeth. "But if you're formally requesting someone else, I'll transfer the assignment to Bishop."

Even if it killed him. But he wasn't leaving the case to Bishop without pressuring the sheriff to call in outside help. When lives were in danger, pride went by the wayside.

"It's just you and Bishop?" she asked, her voice barely more than a whisper. "No one else?"

"Just us two," Liam said. Though the sheriff assisted with cases, he had other duties demanding his attention. Garner also had a ranch on the outskirts of town that took up most of his free time. Unburdened by distractions, Liam was the best choice. "Whatever you think of me, I've never dropped the ball on a case, and I'm not about to start now."

Dallas wasn't a failure. Not yet. Not while there was still breath in his lungs and blood pumping through his veins. He'd make it back if he had to crawl. Swerve had the inside knowledge to take down the top stratum of leadership in the gang. If they cut off the head of the Serpent Brotherhood, the body died. Once that happened, Jenny's death wasn't in vain. He'd go back to his undercover work. His *real* undercover work.

As long as Emma didn't know about his past, she'd never know about his failure.

"Then you have to believe in me," she said, a quiver in her voice. "Really believe in me. Otherwise, this isn't going to work."

He was torn. She sensed his doubts, but he couldn't tell her that this job was temporary. That he was waiting to resurrect the man he'd been in Dallas. That he didn't want to start something he couldn't finish.

"I do my job to the best of my abilities," Liam said. "That I can promise you."

Frustration had him wrapped in knots. The timing was all wrong. After twiddling his thumbs for months, he finally had a reason to stay. He'd simply have to wait and hope that God had a plan for all of them.

"I don't doubt your ability," she said, absently flicking at the blankets on the neatly made bed. "The sheriff told me you were the best man for the job, and I believe him. I also understand that my case is…unique. I understand if that's too much of a challenge."

"I like a challenge," he said, meaning every word. He didn't add that he liked her too, even though he meant those words, as well. "I won't quit until we have answers."

"I believe you. You haven't let me down yet."

Hadn't he?

Her throat worked, and he turned away, giving her a chance to collect herself. She saw him too clearly, and that was dangerous. For both of them. He'd grown accustomed to closing himself off over the years. Another skill he'd learned growing up—how to be invisible. The less he drew attention to himself, the better chance he had of staying in one place for more than a couple of weeks. Invisible kids flew under the radar.

He was the ideal guy to send undercover. People knew him from the old neighborhood, which made him trustworthy, but no one had known him well, which made him anonymous. Jenny's only memory of him was the time he'd prevented Bobby Wilcox from stealing her lunch money. The incident hadn't left much of an impression on her, though. She hadn't even remembered his name. She'd called him "Shiloh" because of the book they were reading in class.

He couldn't share any of that with Emma, but he owed her some sort of explanation.

"My life is complicated right now," he said gruffly. If he wasn't careful, he was going to give away something that risked endangering her further. "I have some unfinished business in another town. I hesitated before because I didn't want to start something I couldn't follow through until the end. No matter what, I'm not leaving until this case is solved."

"Is it personal?" Emma asked, her attention focused on a loose button on her cardigan. "Like a girl?"

"Not a girl." He nearly laughed out loud. Faking his death had been shockingly easy. He'd lost track of the friends he'd had on the police force as a rookie. During his time undercover, the only other person he'd spoken with on a regular basis was his handler. Even clearing out his apartment had been simple. He'd packed a few personal belongings and left his furniture behind. "It's not important."

"We both know that's a lie." She took a step toward him. "I shouldn't have asked about your personal life. That wasn't fair."

Liam took a step backward in an awkward two-step.

"You can ask whatever you want, but I can't always give answers."

"Okay."

Hurt flickered in her beautiful, exotic eyes, and his defenses crumbled. "Look, here's the truth. I'm developing feelings for you, Emma. This has never happened to me before. I don't know what to do. The way things are, what's happening, it's not right. There are things I can't tell you. I'm not who you think I am." The words tumbled from his lips, more words than he ever recalled telling another person about his feelings. More than he'd even been willing to admit to himself. "I'll step aside. You're right. You shouldn't have to deal with everything that's happening and whatever is going on with me. This isn't your problem."

"You're wrong," she said, her voice husky. "This is my problem too, because I feel the same way. I don't know who I am, not fully. But I know how I feel right now. Right here."

She reached for him, and he didn't resist. Of their own volition, his hands moved down her sides and he pulled her flush against him. For once he didn't feel big and awkward. He was strong. Protective. Maybe there was something nurturing inside him after all.

"I feel safe with you," she said, her breath whispering against his skin. "And nowhere else."

She tipped back her head. As he gazed into her stunning topaz eyes, she rose on her tiptoes and kissed him. Hesitant, at first. Softly. Then harder and more insistent. After a brief shock of hesitation, he kissed her back. He slid his palms down her shoulders, cradling her nearer. He kissed her until the room spun and he thought his heart might explode in his chest.

All his life he'd felt out of place. Out of time. *Wrong.* As though he didn't belong anywhere. In that moment, he felt as though he was home. As though there was no other place in the world he belonged but here.

Emma broke the kiss first and pulled back to gaze searchingly into his eyes. For a moment he glimpsed a mirror of his own bittersweet longing. She shook her head at the same doubt and confusion he knew must be swimming there.

"Did you feel that too?" she asked.

He framed her face between his palms and tipped her head up. "Yes, but…"

She held her fingers to his lips. "No. I understand. It's all right."

"There's a lot I can't share with you, Emma," he confessed, torn between wanting to open his heart to her and his duty to the people he'd left behind. The people who'd died because of his secrets. "Things about my life…about myself… I want to…"

Unable to help himself, he bent and touched her lips with his own. The kiss was soft and warm and lingering, a gentle apology.

At a loss, he dropped his hands to his sides.

Shaking her head, she backed away. "Please don't apologize. That only makes it worse."

Dr. Javadi bustled into the room, and Emma spun away.

Liam instantly developed a strange fascination with the gridwork ceiling tiles.

While he waited impatiently, the doctor rattled off instructions and then presented his tablet to Emma. "Signing here states that you understand the instructions of release. If you have worsening headaches, vomiting, seizures, loss of short-term memory, dizziness or increased confusion, return to the emergency room immediately."

A strange emptiness invaded Liam's chest. In Redbird, people knew him and remembered him. Counted on him. Personal relationships made everything more complicated. What was the point of being an invisible man if he didn't have an invisible heart, as well?

"If there's no more paperwork—" Emma gathered her meager belongings "—can we leave now? I need to find out who I am. The sooner the better."

Dr. Javadi smiled, and his features softened. "You know who you are, Ms. Lyons. Your memory simply can't access all the information at the moment. Your brain needs to remake the connections to the past. Nothing about this is going to be neat and tidy."

After reminding Emma once more about the warning signs, the doctor finished up the paperwork and left them alone together.

Liam set his jaw. "Did I mention this was a bad idea?"

After that searing kiss, he wanted more than ever to keep things between them sterile and impersonal, with lots of other people around and the doctor to interrupt if things got too heated.

"You may have alluded." Her topaz eyes took on a faraway look. "Even though I want to go home, I'm not even sure what that is. Not entirely. I wouldn't mind pretending that everything is normal. Except I don't know what normal is anymore."

Normal.

What did that even mean? For either of them. His life back in Dallas was real. Everything that happened in Redbird was a lie. Or was it the other way around? He couldn't tell the difference anymore.

He was playing a part, just like he always did. Or was he?

She waved her hand in a vague circle. "We can just forget about all that other stuff."

He kept thinking of things to say to explain the kiss they'd shared, but all his ideas started with the words "I'm sorry," and she'd said his apology made things worse, which left him without a lot of other choices.

While he hovered in indecision, she reached for a small, wheeled overnight bag that looked vaguely familiar.

He focused his gaze before asking, "Where did that come from?"

"From my car, evidently. Bishop brought it by a day after the accident. Thank goodness he did." She unzipped the shallow front pocket and frowned. "I'd still be wearing the same clothes I had on Friday if he hadn't. The staff made sure everything got washed and dried after the soaking."

She pulled a sheaf of papers from the front pocket and gasped. "Oh, no."

Her fingers went limp and the papers scattered across the floor.

Liam automatically knelt to help her retrieve them. "What is it?"

"Look," she said, scuttling backward.

Fanned across the tile floor were glossy 8 by 10 photographs in perfect condition. No water damage in sight, which meant they'd been placed there after the accident. The images played out like a story. Emma leaving her house, her face blurred through the rain. She was wearing the same navy cardigan and sneakers she'd been wearing the night of the accident. In one photo, she faced the camera, her eyes staring unseeing at the lens.

There was something scrawled across the bottom of the last picture in the stack, and he leaned closer for a better look. His blood turned icy.

Emma whispered the words out loud. "'We aren't finished yet.'"

SEVEN

Emma was numb.

She felt nothing. Not the sunlight she'd desperately craved only hours before. Not the chill spring breeze after the stale hospital air. Nothing. She was detached from the shock of current events. Blissfully, completely numb.

Liam walked beside her, the envelope of photos swinging in his hand. He was taking her home. They'd agreed.

"Do you mind if we make a stop?" he asked. "Won't take long."

A wave of nausea punched her in the gut. "Sure."

She was more frightened than she'd ever been in her life.

"Are you hungry?" he asked. "I'm starving."

She didn't know if she was starving. She couldn't remember the last time she'd eaten.

He was staring at her too closely, and she had to think of an answer. If she didn't say something that made sense soon, he was going to haul her back inside and insist the doctors run more tests. He'd been fussing over her since that kiss. Since the photos.

"Sure," she managed to say, settling on a less-is-more approach.

"How do you feel about Mexican food?"

His words generated a faint stirring of interest. "Okay, I guess."

"There's a great little place in town, and they make the tortillas fresh every morning."

He was waiting for a reply. That's how conversation worked, after all.

She reached for the correct, polite words in return. "That sounds nice."

All Emma wanted to do was curl in a ball and sleep until the pounding in her brain stopped. She wanted only blessed, healing silence.

"Great," he said.

She wasn't hiding her distress very well, and he was clearly worried about her. He was making small talk to nudge her, to see if she was going to crack. She had to put one foot in front of the other until she was miles away from here.

"Great," she repeated blankly.

He slid the envelope with the photos inside his jacket. "Okay."

She didn't protest when he took her bag. All of the items connected to the night of the accident were toxic. Everything—the overnight bag, her totaled car, the hospital. Her memory was spotty at best. She was filling in the edges, but a giant, blank space remained at the center. The blow to her head had left her cruelly handicapped with only random dribbles of recollection surrounding the events leading to the accident.

Who had put them there—and when? They'd been placed there after the accident, that much she knew. She hadn't noticed the zipper pocket before today. She wasn't even certain why she'd checked it beyond a natural curiosity.

Someone had been watching her and wanted her to know she was exposed.

Stumbling, Emma glanced down. The asphalt parking lot was pitted and in need of repair.

As Liam led the way to his truck, he paused to retrieve his sunglasses from his breast pocket.

She brushed past the deputy, picking up speed. She needed distance between her and the envelope. The photos were like a live, breathing thing—a telltale heart thumping beneath his jacket.

"Stop." He jogged to catch up. "What's wrong?"

"Nothing," she snapped bitterly without turning around. "I'm fine."

He let go of the bag and easily caught up to her, then blocked her path. "You're not fine. Talk to me."

Glancing behind her, she blanched. She was caught between those photos and that awful, suffocating hospital room.

"I'm sorry," Liam said, his expression awash with guilt. "You have every right to be angry. We were supposed to keep you safe, and we didn't."

"I don't blame you." The empty and emotionless words came by rote. "Everyone did their best. I'm here, aren't I? I survived the accident. I survived the attack."

She'd survived because someone out there wanted her to. He wanted her alive because he had worse things in store for her. This was all part of an elaborate, cruel game, and she was playing right into the killer's hands.

The bullets and the photos were merely parlor tricks designed to scare her. They were the work of a cheap sideshow carny. Her stalker was giving her sly nudges to let her know she wasn't safe. Not here. Not now. Maybe not ever. He was letting her know there were *no* gaps in *his* memory of her. How much more did he know about her than she knew about herself?

A surge of anger sputtered to life inside her.

Liam was blocking her path to the truck, and she scooted around him. "I'm not going back into that hospital."

"Okay."

"He had photos of me." She pivoted on her heel and violently gestured with one arm. "He was watching me."

"I know," Liam said, his arms raised in a supplicating gesture, the corner of the envelope visible beneath his jacket. "I'm sorry."

Staring at those pictures slammed home the reckless danger of her situation. She didn't remember that night.

He remembered, though.

He was hunting her.

"I feel violated." The air was too close, and her clothing was smothering her. She clawed at her sweater and tossed the material to the ground. "He knows where I live. How can I go home? He was right outside, and I never saw him."

The chill air washed over the bare skin of her arms. What else had she missed? Where else had her stalker followed? She scanned the parking lot, the tree-lined railroad tracks in the distance, the reflective windows of the hospital and the highway rumbling past. Was he watching her now?

Liam took a cautious step toward her, and hysterical laughter bubbled in the back of her throat. He must think she was crazy. She felt crazy. She was out of control, careening toward a danger she didn't recognize and couldn't identify.

Her stomach pitched, and her skin grew clammy. "I don't feel good. I feel like I'm shaking on the inside. I don't feel right."

No, no, no. This wasn't happening.

She stumbled away, but he was too quick.

He tenderly hauled her against him. Slipping his thumb beneath her jaw, he tipped her face up and bent his head until their foreheads were touching.

"You're all right," he murmured gently. "He's not here. Let it go."

His deep voice vibrated against her skin, and his arms were strong and safe. She wanted nothing more than to sink into the comfort of his shelter, but he couldn't be trusted. Not entirely. His beard brushed her cheek as she turned away. He thought that four walls and a door might keep her safe, but she knew better.

She jerked away from him, her face white, as much from shock as anger at the situation. "I'm not going back inside there."

Liam didn't turn a hair at her outburst, further stoking her rage. She'd rent a motel room. She'd go to the next town. She wasn't going home, and she wasn't going back to the hospital, either.

"No one is taking you anywhere you don't want to go," Liam asserted. "You don't have to do anything you don't want to do."

He took her hands in his. The rough pads of his thumbs smoothed back and forth over the delicate bones, distracting her from her terror. She still felt strange—achy and unsettled—and she had to do battle against an inexplicable urge to scream her frustration.

"Do you promise?" She stared at the corner of the envelope, and a suffocating rage consumed her. "Don't lie to me."

Whatever he was about to say caught in his throat. He glanced away but not before she saw a look she knew too well. *Guilt.*

"I'm not lying to you about this," he said finally, letting his hands fall away.

The look of guilt worsened, and the implication landed like a wall between them. Alarm bells rang in her head, and she took a cautious step backward.

"Then you've lied to me already."

"Not about this," he repeated, and his mask of detachment slipped. "About my past."

His admission drained all the fight from her. There were things he couldn't share with her; he'd said that already. She barely remembered her own past. How could she fault him for withholding his? None of this was his fault. She'd done this to herself. Somehow or another, she'd unleashed a monster.

His expression flattened, and she sensed he was bracing for her anger. In an odd sort of way, his brutal honesty had put them on equal footing. Whether by accident or by design, they both had parts of their past they couldn't share with each other.

"Don't worry." Her voice shook so much she could barely speak, and the words came in a ragged whisper. "I don't even know my own secrets. How can I be critical of yours?"

A wave of exhaustion rippled through her, and her hands found their way across the space between them. Her world had been filled with danger and fear and so much uncertainty that she'd spent her last waking hours in a constant state of panic. There was nothing wrong with seeking a moment of peace, and that was one thing Liam had always provided.

He didn't protest when she wrapped her arms around him, inhaling his spicy male scent and the memories associated with it. That first night, he'd refused to give up even when saving her life meant risking his own. If he withheld parts of himself from her, that was a price she was willing to pay.

For now, she trusted him. If he said he wasn't taking her back to the hospital, then he wasn't.

"Why?" She lifted her head and gazed at him, her face wet. "Why is this happening?"

"I don't know," he said quietly.

His honesty comforted her more than false platitudes. She slumped against him and he pulled her closer, wrapping her tightly in his embrace.

"He could be anywhere." As long as he was out there, she'd never be safe. She needed to take back her power. She needed to feel in control of something. She needed Liam to understand what was happening to her. "He knows me."

"He doesn't know you." Liam brushed her cheek with the back of his knuckles. "He doesn't know anything about you."

Her body spasmed with uncontrollable shivering. "He could be watching right now. How do we know he's not?"

"Don't give him the edge. He wants you distracted because that makes you an easier target. Don't let him inside your head."

"How can I stop him?" she asked in a voice that wasn't quite as steady as she would have liked. "I can't even get into my own head. There are so many gaps."

"And you're filling in those gaps all the time." He held her slightly away from him, forcing her to meet his silvery blue eyes. "He's shattered your trust. He's taken away the things that make you feel safe. You can't change that, but you have a decision to make. You can be a victim, or you can be both a victim and a survivor."

"Aren't you supposed to say, 'or'?" She felt wretched—defensive and angry and oddly guilty over her loss memory. "You can be a victim *or* a survivor?"

"It's never that easy, is it? No one can take away what he's done to you, but you can survive this. You'll be different, but that's okay. Different doesn't have to be better or worse. We survive, or we surrender."

"I remember looking in the mirror that first morning and being comforted by the thought that God knew who I was even if I didn't, but my faith has been shaken since then." A dart of panic lanced through her. "Do you ever wonder if God is blind to our suffering?"

"All the time." His mouth quirked in a lopsided grin, and he sighed. "When I have doubts, I remember that it's times like these when we strengthen our bond with Him. Because if we don't have faith, what else do we have?"

Faith was a matter of trust, and her trust had been chipped away these past few days. "What about those eighteen unsolved murders in the Killing Fields? All that needless misery. The victims. Their families and friends. There's so much grief, I can't even wrap my head around the loss."

Their faces crept into her dreams. They were searching for answers she didn't have. The task she'd set for herself was impossible.

"God never said there'd be no suffering," Liam said. "He only promised to fill our suffering with purpose."

She wanted to give the victims of those crimes a voice. She wanted them to be more than faceless names and statistics. She wanted to give their suffering meaning. Was that even possible?

"Do you really think so?"

He dropped a kiss on her mouth before cupping the back of her head with his enormous hand and holding her tightly against his thundering heart. "I know so."

They were only words, but she was glad to have them. Grateful for something to hold on to besides the fear and uncertainty.

Liam rocked her gently, murmuring soothing words, his warm breath rustling against her hair. She teetered on the edge, afraid if she let herself cry, truly cry—not these tears leaking from her eyes—if she truly gave in, she might never return.

She didn't know how long they stayed like that or how long they might have stayed that way if the deputy's stomach hadn't rumbled.

The sound drew a reluctant grin from her. He was hungry. With everything else happening around them, there were practical matters to consider. The mundane tasks of eating and sleeping went right alongside living and dying.

For days, a dangerous stranger had left her feeling as though she was prey—that she was being hunted. No more.

"I'm sorry," she said shakily, acutely embarrassed by her loss of control. "I don't know what happened just now. I guess I sort of lost it. You brought me back. Thank you."

"All I did was remind you that you're a strong person. You're a survivor. You don't need your memory to know that. You don't even need me to remind you. You'll get through this."

Her chest tightened. Their time together was temporary; he'd made that clear. There were things in his past he wasn't willing to share. He had responsibilities in another town. He'd set the boundaries, though they'd both broken the rules.

Not that she regretted the kiss. On the contrary, she was grateful to know him, at least for the short time they had together. Some people were like that, she supposed. Some people drifted into a life on the tide and left the same way, but that didn't mean they weren't important.

"We should eat," she said. "We're both hungry."

Part of being strong was getting on with the business of living. Her path going forward was crystal clear.

If survival or surrender were the choices, then she chose survival.

* * *

Liam watched the play of emotions. The crisis was passing. Emma was strong, and she was going to need that strength. There'd be good days and bad days ahead, but she'd always have this moment to fall back on.

She'd always have the moment she decided to survive rather than surrender.

He turned and walked the few steps to her bag and grasped the handle. "Are you ready?" he asked without looking up.

"I'm ready." When she reached the truck, she tossed back her head and thrust out her arms. "Some days it's enough just to be alive, isn't it?"

Her topaz eyes shimmered with vibrant emotion, and his pulse stuttered. He thought of the other guys he'd worked with showing him pictures on their phones, how they'd changed over the years—from solitary hunting trips to family vacations. Would the pictures on his phone ever change?

He ducked his head, afraid the pain and longing were evident. That sort of thinking was a dead end. If he stayed, he'd have to tell her about Dallas. She didn't know the real man. She knew the deputy—so far.

"It's good to be alive," he said. She'd have the illusion instead of the truth. It was better that way. For both of them. He stowed her bag, assisted her into the passenger seat, then got behind the wheel and dropped the truck into gear. "There's a dock on the lake. We have time to stop, if you'd like. Won't add more than fifteen minutes to the trip. The view is peaceful there."

Part of coming to Redbird was the chance to get his head straight. He knew just the place to offer a respite.

"I'd like that," she answered softly. "I could use a little peace."

The route was circuitous. They'd have to pass through the town to reach the lake, then circle back for lunch, but he figured the drive would do her good. Nothing like a little fresh air to clear a guy's head.

Slowing for a red light, he considered Redbird with new eyes. "We'll drive through downtown before we pass by B&B row, then it's not much farther to the lake."

Emma rolled down the window and let the chill wind ruffle her hair. "What's B&B row?"

He'd never been asked to play tour guide before, but he was warming up to the role. "A river cuts right through the center of town. Gives the place a different look than a lot of other Texas towns. An enterprising entrepreneur got the bright idea to dam off the river and create a rec-reational oasis outside of town." He'd miss the lake when he went back to Dallas. There was nothing like casting a line on a spring day to clear a guy's head. "We get a lot of tax income to keep the place looking nice. There are a few mansions around the lake. Summer homes for the rich who come up from Austin or drive from Dallas. But the park service also maintains five boat ramps and two fish-ing piers for us regular folks."

"Sounds lovely," she said. "You know it's funny, I re-member looking for houses on the internet, but I can't remember why I chose to live in Redbird. Maybe it was the lake."

"Maybe."

Swiveling to face him, she asked, "Then it's a tour-ist town?"

"Mostly. It's crowded during the summer, although we get plenty of traffic all year round. The town square is filled with what you'd expect. Antiques shops, bakeries and a used bookstore. Quaint, Americana kind of stuff."

"That doesn't explain the bed-and-breakfasts. Why stay in town if there's a lake nearby?"

"A national magazine featured Redbird as the ideal destination for ladies' groups." Liam hadn't realized until now how much of the history he'd absorbed in his short time here. "The notoriety kicked off a need for smaller, homier hotels. The locals bought up some of the Victorian houses in the center of town and refurbished them. There must be almost a dozen bed-and-breakfasts. From what I've seen, the town gets a lot of book clubs, church groups and the occasional tame bachelorette party."

He wasn't normally a talker, but the light, innocuous chatter kept both their minds off their troubles

"Seems like a busy place," she said. "Why only a single sheriff and two deputies for all those people?"

"The town has its own police force, and we patrol the lake and surrounding areas. Land that isn't incorporated. The average age of the residents is higher than in the cities. Not much happens around here. Haven't had a murder in twenty years. We're too far from the border to worry about the drug trade." He cast a sharp glance in her direction, searching for any reaction to his words. Her expression remained curious and impassive. "Church groups and book clubs aren't known for needing a lot of police intervention," he continued. "Mostly it's nuisance calls."

"Have you lived here all your life?"

"No." He barked out a laugh. "I didn't grow up here. I'm from Dallas."

That city was enormous. There was no harm in admitting the truth. There was no chance their paths were ever going to cross after this.

He was growing accustomed to her natural curiosity. While his instinct was to react defensively, he was beginning to understand that her questions were part of her need to understand and make sense of the world around her. Where he closed himself off, Emma drew people toward her.

His radio crackled, giving him a good excuse to end the conversation. While he didn't mind her interest, he still hadn't grown accustomed to personal questions. Since he mostly kept to himself, he hadn't needed the practice.

"Unit 120," he said. "Go ahead."

"Royce Williams is calling to report a suspicious package on his porch," Rose said.

That was the third time this month. "Ask Royce if the package says 'Amazon' on the outside."

"Ten-four." A pause. "Affirmative. The package says 'Amazon' on the outside."

"Have Royce ask Barbara if she ordered something from Amazon."

Another long pause. "Royce says never mind."

"Ten-four."

Emma laughed. "Does that happen often?"

"Often enough."

"If you didn't grow up here, what brought you to the town?"

"The job."

He glanced at her profile and his breath caught. The wind had whipped her hair around her shoulders and brought a flush of color to her cheeks.

Getting her out of the hospital was the right choice. She was sweet and brave and vulnerable, and he wanted to protect her from anything that might hurt her. He wanted to hold her in his arms and shelter her, but all that was useless if he couldn't see her smile. The reprieve had brought a much-needed buoyancy to her mood.

He gestured to an elaborate stone building with a

cupola in the center of a well-manicured green space. "That's the county courthouse."

The town really wasn't that bad, all things considered. He thought he'd miss the Dallas nightlife until he remembered he rarely went out. He hadn't dated seriously in years. There'd been one relationship in college he'd thought might go somewhere. She'd soon made it clear that he was only a diversion before she settled down with someone from her dad's country club. He'd been more careful to keep his feelings disentangled after that experience. He was the guy women used as a distraction, not the one they married.

"What a beautiful town," Emma said.

"It's all right, I guess."

Rose's voice sounded over the speaker, and he replied with his call number out of habit. "Go ahead."

"I've got a request for a welfare check on Artie Druckerman." Rose rattled off the address. "Deputy Bishop is checking it out, but I thought you should know, as well, because there's more. Apparently, no one has seen his dog, either."

That piqued Liam's interest "Any chance his dog is a rust-colored Pomeranian named Duchess?"

Emma made a noise, but when he glanced over, she looked away.

"That's mighty specific," Rose said. "I'll ask around."

"All right. Let me know what Bishop discovers." He glanced at the clock. The dog was due to have puppies. People were fanatic about their pets around here. "We should be prepared for the worst."

"Ten-four."

Liam made a note on the pad of paper attached to his dashboard to follow up. He turned onto a tree-lined boulevard featuring facing rows of Victorian houses. Several of them sported swinging signs in the front yard advertising quaint names like Sylvan House and Peaceful Haven.

"B&B row," Liam said. "Do you want to drive past your house?"

"Not just yet." She pressed her hands against her cheeks. "I keep thinking about my attacker watching me. Taking pictures. It's awful knowing that he remembers and I don't."

"Then we'll skip it for now."

He took the curve past town and snuck a glance at her face as the highway arced toward the lake. She was staring through the windshield and wearing a look that worried him.

"What's wrong?"

Her eyebrows were drawn together, her forehead creased in thought, and her expression was hard. "There's a connection to this place. I moved here for a reason. To be closer to something."

His heartbeat stalled. "Or someone?"

"No. Something happened here, but I don't know what."

"The doctor said not to force it," he replied, more relieved than he had a right to be. "You've already remembered a lot. It'll come back."

"I suppose. But it's frustrating and unsettling."

"Then let's fill in the space with some good memories."

He never tired of this view. The scenery changed as they neared the lake, becoming softer and lusher. The trees were taller and sturdier and planted closer together. There were times after a bad day when he'd round the corner and feel the tension drain from his body. He kept a fishing pole in the back, and sometimes he'd drop a line with no bait. No one bothered a guy when he was fishing, and he enjoyed the solitude.

Today, he didn't mind the company.

Most people didn't know about the dock at the north end of the lake. Even at the height of the tourist season, the area remained mostly deserted. He took the service road, enjoying the sound of his tires crunching over the gravel.

He parked and circled around to open Emma's door, grasping her fingers to help her down from the tall seat.

"You don't have to treat me with kid gloves," she said. "I won't break."

"I know."

He didn't mention that he appreciated feeling useful to another person. Nor did he mention that he liked the way she leaned into him and grasped his shoulder when he helped her down, or the way her light, floral scent mingled with the breeze off the lake.

"It's beautiful here," she said, gazing at the crystal expanse of still water visible through the trees. "It's like we've traveled to another time and place, and we've only come a few miles from town."

"I know the feeling."

In Dallas, the same distance separated million-dollar mansions from the boarded-up and blighted neighborhoods of the city. He was less than a day's drive from his old life, but the distance might as well have been halfway to the moon. Some things weren't worth thinking too hard about.

Clouds drifted over the sun, and a chill wind stirred up the water.

He shrugged out of his coat and draped it over her shoulders. "Why don't you walk to the end? The dock is safe, don't worry. I test it just about once a week when I'm fishing."

She flashed him a grateful smile, brushing his fingers with hers as she adjusted the material.

He wasn't a sentimental man, but there was a time of evening at the lake when the sky faded at the edges, and the noises grew hushed. People naturally drifted back to their homes for dinner, leaving the surface a glassy reflection of the sky. The water seemed to purify the air, leaving the scents surrounding him fresh and clean.

Twilight at the lake was his favorite time of day.

Letting the scenery work its magic, he gave her a few minutes of solitude before he hopped onto the dock and joined her.

"This is so peaceful," she said, her gaze fixed on the expanse of water.

"Yes," he replied, his attention focused on the delicate curve of her neck visible where she'd tucked her hair behind one ear.

"I almost forgot," she said. "Deputy Bishop said you should look into case file 1701."

Liam didn't bother hiding his shock. "When did you speak with Bishop?"

"Last night." She captured her billowing hair against her neck. "It was the stupidest thing. I thought the door to my room was locked, and I nearly panicked. He must have thought I was crazy."

A burning fear welled inside him, and Liam touched her arm. "Be careful around him."

"Bishop? Why?"

"I can't tell you exactly." He made a mental note to call the sheriff. Until this was over, he didn't want Bishop anywhere near Emma. "It's best if you rely on me and Sheriff Garner."

"Okay."

Grateful for her easy capitulation, he said, "We should be getting back."

They turned from the lake and made their way to the truck. He took her hand and helped her jump from the dock to the shore. Her hair caught the breeze and snagged on the placket of his shirt.

Their gazes met and clashed, and a silent battle raged within him. He'd never felt such a confusing mix of emotions for a woman. There was passion, but there was also tenderness and caring. There was a fierce possessiveness to his thoughts that was entirely foreign.

The long-range plans he'd made for his life had come to an abrupt halt in the sweltering Dallas heat as the sirens had sounded in the distance. Even before Jenny's death, his goals had always been work-related. He'd make the next promotion, he'd get the next pay raise. He'd put money in the bank and keep his needs simple because money meant security. His personal life had begun and ended with eating well and staying in shape.

He was old-fashioned at heart. Love meant marriage and family. He had no road map for that kind of life.

Emma reached up and freed the strands of her hair caught on his shirt. He held his breath until she turned away.

With a last look over his shoulder, he savored the moment. His life was in Dallas, not here. Even if he managed to save Emma, he'd never be able to bring Jenny back. He'd tried to protect her, and he'd gotten her killed instead. The weight of his past mistakes threatened to crush him.

"There's something," Emma said, tugging him back from the past. "I know this place, I feel it. Do you mind if I just wait here for a few minutes? See if something comes back?"

"Not at all."

Memories of a night he never wanted to relive flooded his thoughts. When he left Redbird, he'd be leaving Emma behind, but he'd also be leaving Deputy Liam McCourt behind. He'd miss the man he'd created because he was starting to like this rendition of himself. Except this version wasn't real.

The darkness he'd hoped to bury shrouded him. Leaving was better because she'd eventually see through the illusion. He couldn't handle it if Emma thought getting close to him was a mistake. He didn't want to stick around for the disappointment in her eyes.

She gripped his arm, her fingers digging painfully into his skin. "I can go home now."

Her expression sent his heart pounding. "Why?"

"Because I remember now. I remember everything."

EIGHT

Drowning in a flood of memories, Emma clutched her head in her hands. After her startling announcement, she'd insisted on leaving at once. The scenery outside the windows flew by, and she slanted forward, as though she could speed up the insight into her past.

"We came here as kids." She pulled her palms down her face. "This is where we vacationed each summer. We found a body. Me and my stepbrother."

The dream finally made sense. They hadn't gotten in trouble. The reaction had merely been a childish response to the situation. Jordan had shielded her from the worst of the horror, but he hadn't been able to hide everything. She'd caught a glimpse of the woman's pale, limp hands, her torn fingernails and bound wrists, before running away. Jordan's dad had claimed he discovered the body to shield them from the attention. He'd wanted to keep their names out of the press.

"Wait a second." His eyes on the road, Liam flashed his hand. "Slow down. A body? Like a dead body?"

Staring into the stagnant water near the dock, the past had merged with the present in the blink of an eye.

"I'm trying to put everything in order." She'd been exhausted before, but the return of her memories had given her a renewed burst of energy. "When Rose said the name Artie Druckerman, I knew I'd heard it before. Then, when I looked back at the lake just now, everything shifted. It was like a flash of lightning. For the oddest fraction of a second, everything came rushing back. *Everything.* All the pieces just came together."

"What about Artie?"

"I was working with him on something. He might have information."

Liam radioed dispatch and learned that Bishop had checked the house and there was no sign of Artie.

"We'll keep trying. What you've remembered is good. But you gotta let me catch up. Why don't we stop someplace and sort this all out. You said you like Mexican food, right?"

"I love Mexican food!"

She loved anything and everything now that she remembered. As she strove to bring order to the rush of memories, Liam drove them to a quaint restaurant where they requested an isolated booth toward the back so they wouldn't be disturbed.

Emma wanted to order everything on the menu even though she wasn't certain she was hungry anymore. She finally settled on a combination platter and a sweet tea.

"I don't know where to start," she said the moment the waiter was out of earshot.

Liam smiled at her enthusiasm, but his smile quickly dimmed. "Give yourself a minute. How are you holding up?"

"Overwhelmed. I know I've only been out of commission for a few days." She tapped her foot and traced the decorative pattern carved into the table. "You realize how fragile life is. Losing my memory was terrifying and isolating. Our whole lives are based on feelings and memories, and we're nothing when that's gone."

"I disagree," he assured her kindly. "Your personality was there. Your heart never changed."

Her cheeks heated. "I wanted to thank you for what you said the other night. When you said that kids are jerks sometimes. I can't tell you how long I've been carrying that burden."

"It has to do with the dream, doesn't it? What you said in the truck about you and your stepbrother discovering a body."

"Yes. It was the first summer after my mom married my stepdad. I wasn't getting along with Jordan. I was mad that she'd chosen to bring them here. This was our place. I wanted something that was just ours. Me and my..."

Her throat closed around the words. Her emotions were ricocheting all over the map.

"You and your dad?" Liam prompted.

"I barely remember him," she managed to choke out as she wrestled for control of her sorrow. She'd dealt with all this stuff years ago. Except her feelings refused to listen to logic. "I'd ask my mom about him all the time. She'd tell me the story of how they met." All at once Emma was spinning and spinning down a cyclone of memories. "They were in college together. He'd had leukemia as a child, but he'd been in remission for years. I was three when he was diagnosed again. He lost that battle. A few years later, my mom remarried, and she stopped telling me stories. I was so angry. I hated her new husband for that. I blamed him for taking my dad away from me. For taking my mom away from me, too."

"That must have been rough."

Her heart pitched, and she stared, unseeing, at the colorful sombrero quivering in the gentle breeze of the ceiling fan above them. "Things got better after I left home. When mom quit work, I didn't think anything of it. My stepdad had to call me. She'd been diagnosed with something called pulmonary hypertension, only she didn't want to worry me while I was in college." Emma kept her head tipped upward, blinking to capture her tears. "I had to forgive him after that, didn't I? He took care of her until the end. I can't believe how naive I was. I thought they'd find a cure or something. I couldn't believe God would take both of my parents."

Sniffling, she studied the decorative pattern on the table once more. It seemed odd, revealing such tragic personal things in such a whimsical setting. Odd and somehow right, too. No matter what was happening in her life, the rest of the world was going about its business. That knowledge kept her grounded. Somewhere else, someone was having a perfectly mundane day.

Liam adjusted the napkin-wrapped silverware. "I'm sorry about your mom and dad."

"What about your parents?" she asked, attempting to distract herself from the tears that were about to explode in her eyes. "Do they live in Dallas?"

"They're gone." Melancholy shimmered in his expression and gentled the rough texture of his voice. "My dad was never in my life anyway. By the time I was old enough to look for him, he was dead and buried. I don't remember much of my mom. She overdosed when I was little."

Though she felt guilty for asking, Emma was absurdly grateful for his honesty. "I'm sorry. I shouldn't have asked."

"You have every right to ask questions. If I don't want to answer, I'll say so."

"We all have crosses to bear, don't we? At least I had my mom for a while. I have those memories." She pressed the heels of her hands against her eyes. "I don't know what's come over me. The memories are all tangled with my feelings, and I can't seem to separate the two."

"Then don't try. We'll take things slow."

"I can't though, can I? He's out there right now. Watching me."

"Who? Can you remember—"

The waiter appeared, and they fell silent as he delivered their drinks.

When he'd vanished around the corner once more, Liam shifted in his seat. "Do you remember who ran you off the road?"

Her head started spinning and the edges of her vision turned gray, giving her tunnel vision.

"I don't know," she panted.

She felt as though she couldn't breathe, as though she was suffocating.

"Relax. Stop trying to remember."

It was a struggle even to speak. "Why can I remember everything else but not that day?" She refused to succumb to the anxiety welling inside her. "What's wrong with me?"

"Nothing is wrong with you." Liam reached across the table and took her hand. "This is something I understand. I see it all the time with car accidents. People lose the period around a traumatic event. The doctor even warned us this might happen."

Saying the word *us* was like tossing her an anchor against the drowning panic. Knowing he'd be by her side throughout the process eased some of her concerns. She'd be facing the unknown, but she wouldn't be alone.

"Really? This is normal? You're sure? Because I thought everything was going to be all right and now I'm not so certain. What if I lose my memory all over again?"

"You won't lose what you've gained. I may not be a doctor, but I understand trauma. I promise you, what you're experiencing is the most normal thing that's happened all week."

Liam released her hand and ran his finger down the condensation of his glass.

"How can you know for sure?" she whispered, afraid of saying the words any louder.

Afraid of slipping into the void once more.

"Because it happened to me once," he said, his voice tired and a little guilty. "I lost a couple days after an accident."

"What happened?" she blurted, her curiosity overtaking her good manners.

Rude or not, it was a natural question considering his admission.

"I was shot." He motioned. "Left shoulder."

Shock flowed through her. Emma searched him as though she might see a sign of his injury. "But you're okay? I'm assuming you were on duty?"

"Yeah." He took a drink from his glass, the surface of the water rippling in his unsteady hand. "I was working undercover. I thought I was good at my job, but I made a mistake. I did something that made someone suspicious."

"What?" she asked automatically, then wanted to kick herself for asking such a pointed question. He was upset, and she was pushing him. "This is what I do for a living. I ask questions. It's natural for me, but it can be…unsettling for other people."

"That's all right. It doesn't matter what I did. I messed up. Gave myself away. It nearly cost the whole undercover operation."

He appeared to regret the damage to his police work more than getting shot.

"You might have died," she said.

His eyes were filled with regret and something else… Shame. "I didn't."

"I'm glad you didn't, or I wouldn't be here."

He opened his mouth to say something, then appeared to change his mind. "You're strong. Another couple of minutes and you'd have saved yourself."

She wanted to protest, to offer more assurance, but their entrées came. For the next few moments, they were distracted by the rituals of arranging plates and silverware and answering the waiter's questions before Liam continued.

"I went through some rehab," he said. "But I'm feeling good now. I got a job here to get my head straight."

"How's that working out for you so far?" The question came out more flippant than she'd intended, and she cringed, "I mean, are you fully recovered?"

None of this was coming out right. He'd been so closed off before, she wanted to wedge open his revelations. He'd mentioned unfinished business in Dallas, and it must have something to do with the shooting—with blowing his cover. Was he on some sort of forced leave? She wanted answers, but she sensed he'd said all he had to say on the subject, and the unknown left her frustrated.

"Things are coming together." He cleared his throat. "I'm good."

"Thank you for telling me," she said.

"It's all right. Just don't mention any of this to anyone else, okay?" Weary resignation etched his features. "No one here knows about my past, and I'd prefer to keep it that way."

He'd given her insight into himself to ease her worry, and she appreciated his sacrifice. She didn't doubt the admission had cost him. He was a master of detachment. He'd told her everything and, at the same time, he'd told her nothing.

He was right about the accident and the forgetting—none of that had altered her personality. She wasn't the sort of person who lived easily with a mystery, and Liam

McCourt would always be a puzzle with missing pieces. Not the sort of person she was compatible with.

Some women liked the simple, uncomplicated attraction of a love 'em and leave 'em kind of guy. Emma wasn't one of them. These past few days had left her raw and vulnerable, her emotions lacerated. They'd also given her a sense of perspective.

Life was too short to waste on casual affairs that were bound to go nowhere. Though she didn't regret what had passed between them, she'd keep her distance from now on. She wanted someone in her life who was going to be there for the long haul, and Liam didn't fit the bill.

Though her initial adjustment had been difficult, she adored Redbird. When she thought of Dallas, it was a jumble of suffocating summer heat and the crush of people. She'd discovered a kinder version of herself away from all that, and she wasn't ready to give up on her better self.

She snorted softly. Not that he'd asked.

Eager to connect with Artie now that she recalled talking to him before, she concentrated on eating, or at least pushing her food around her plate as though she was eating.

Liam appeared to be doing the same.

He set down his fork and slumped against the back of the booth. "Let's revisit what you remember. How do you know Artie?"

"After I moved back here, that summer was never far from my mind." According to Jordan, she'd always been obsessed. Living near the scene of the crime had exacerbated her interest. "As a kid, my mom assured me that the woman's killer had been caught. Mom wanted me to feel safe again. When I started looking into the case after I moved to Redbird, I realized things weren't quite as cut and dried as she led me to believe."

"How do you mean?" he asked, his face tight.

"They pinned her murder on a drifter. They caught him a few towns over, and he confessed. Except he'd gotten all the details wrong. I know, because I was there, and Jordan had seen her. We'd talk about that day sometimes. The man who confessed was wrong about what she was wearing, about the place she was found. I started looking into the statistics, and false confessions happen all the time." Maybe Jordan wasn't that far off in his accusations of her obsession. The case had consumed her thoughts. "I was doing some research at the Redbird Library, and the librarian suggested I contact Artie. He's been digitizing all the archived issues of the Redbird *Gazette*. I never met him in person. I called him. He said he'd look for information on the case. Local stories. That sort of thing."

Liam drummed his fingers on the table. "Are you working on anything else? Any other articles for the *Dallas Morning News*?"

"No. I was finishing up my book on the Lonestar State Killer." She snapped her fingers. "'Unforgotten.' That's the working title. I knew that word meant something. It's been nagging me all week."

"And nothing else? Nothing on Mexican cartels?"

"No." She made a face. "That's not my area of expertise."

"Any death threats?"

"No."

"Okay. So, you're not writing about drug dealers and you haven't gotten any death threats."

She didn't know why he kept focusing on the Mexican cartels. "No."

"I found Duchess late Friday afternoon," he mused. "About the time you'd have been packing to leave."

As she recalled the earlier radio call, a wild surge of

panic raced through her. "Artie is missing. That's what Rose said. I was so distracted by getting my memory back, I forgot all about what kicked this off."

"Someone requested a wellness check, that's all. That doesn't necessarily mean anything is wrong, just that he's been out of touch. I'll check his house again. See if there's something that might indicate where he's gone. Ask around."

"I'm going with you," she shot back.

Dread weighed on her chest. Now that her memory had returned, she was heavily invested in Artie's fate, and she had a bad feeling about his continued absence. What had Artie discovered?

Liam didn't argue. "Okay. But we do it my way."

"Agreed."

Artie was the key to unraveling the mystery surrounding who wanted her dead.

Liam suspected that Artie had either discovered something incriminating and scampered, or someone had silenced him. He was certain the dog was Artie's. Call it instinct. There was no way Artie had left his dog unclaimed since Friday. Not a purebred with a litter of puppies on the way. Artie probably loved Duchess, and he wouldn't let her wander around the town square.

Unwilling to disappoint Emma when she was celebrating the return of her memory, he kept his suspicions to himself. Since Bishop had already checked out the house, he was confident Artie had met his fate—whatever that might be—elsewhere.

The trip didn't take long. Artie's house was a battered white two-story shotgun a couple of blocks off Main Street. Liam peered through the windows, but the shades were drawn. He ran his fingers around the window flashing and was rewarded for his effort. Artie wasn't very imaginative when it came to hiding his extra key.

Emma hovered behind him, and he faced her. "Wait in the foyer. I need to check the house first."

Better to be safe than sorry, just in case Bishop had missed something.

"Is this legal?"

"Someone called in a wellness check. The door was open."

"You opened it."

"Details."

He unlocked the door and his senses were assailed with a musty shock. The place was stacked floor to ceiling with books and teetering piles of newspaper, limiting his visibility. There were no telltale signs that Artie was here—alive or otherwise—though he wasn't taking any chances.

Emma surveyed the jumble. "This is hopeless. How are we ever going to find anything in this place?"

"Wait here," he ordered.

There'd been too many close calls in the past few days.

She rolled her eyes. "Yes. Go. Hurry up. If we're going to find anything, we'd better get started."

Liam made quick work of searching the house, but there was no sign of Artie. He allowed himself a moment of relief before returning downstairs. He'd half expected to discover a crime scene.

The man's disappearance meant they had their work cut out for them. As many books as Artie had in the front room, there were floor-to-ceiling bookshelves lining the space that must have served as a dining room when the house was originally built. Paths had been carved through the towering mounds in a bizarre maze.

The overhead lights were yellowed with age and barely brightened the task. Dusty, threadbare curtains hung in the windows, revealing shafts of light illuminating the swirling dust motes their movements kicked up. Cobwebs stretched between the corners of the ceiling and dangled to the tops of the shelves. The whole claustrophobic atmosphere was straight out of a horror movie.

Emma shuddered and shook her arms. "This place could be in an episode on a TV show about hoarders."

"Look at this first."

She followed him into the kitchen, and her eyes widened.

"Yep," he said. "That was my reaction."

Though the counters were crowded with more papers and books, the floor was immaculate. Checkerboard black-and-white floor tiles gleamed in the artificial light. A pristine dog bed took up one corner, with a bowl of food placed next to a basket of colorful chew toys.

The sorrow in her topaz eyes mirrored his own.

She shook her head. "He's not coming back, is he?"

"This doesn't look good."

Her distress tugged at something deep in his chest. She brought out every protective instinct he had, and some he hadn't known he possessed before now. When he'd alluded to his past in the restaurant, she hadn't looked at him in disgust. Then again, he hadn't told her the whole story.

She was still wearing his jacket. More like swimming in it. She'd rolled back the sleeves, and the hem nearly reached her knees. The sight was oddly intimate. He pictured them in high school, exchanging class rings while she wore his letterman jacket. Too bad he hadn't been a letterman jacket kind of student. He doubted she'd have worn the ratty leather coat he'd inherited from one of his foster brothers.

Chiding himself for the maudlin, Oliver Twist turn

of his thoughts, he moved away. "Why don't you look around? See if anything jumps out at you."

"We don't even know what we're looking for."

"No. But we might as well try."

They returned to the dining room and stood in confused silence, neither of them knowing quite where to begin.

Liam tilted his head to the side and studied the spines of the books at his eye level. "I'll give him one thing. As messy as this place looks, I think he must have had some sort of organization. These books are alphabetized."

Emma stepped closer, her breath whispering against his neck. "You're right. He must have had some sort of system."

Her floral scent drifted over him, and his breathing grew uneven.

"Still doesn't help us." His gaze scuttled across her lips, and he searched for a diversion. "You said he was digitizing the old newspapers. He must have a computer. Something he uses for scanning. I didn't see anything on my first search of the house."

"Well, let's try to think like Artie. There was something he wanted to show me. Something he'd dug up in the archives when he was digitizing the newspapers."

"Check around. I'll do another search for a computer or a scanner."

Liam was drifting into another one of those gray areas. This wasn't, technically, a legal search.

Emma turned in a slow circle. "All right. If I was Artie, where would I put something that I was working on? Something important."

They spent an hour searching the stacks of books and newspapers downstairs. Liam opened all the cupboards and even dug through the dog bed. His fingertips turned gray, and dusty patches showed on his knees.

Emma sneezed and swiped at her nose. "I'm going to check upstairs."

"Bless you." He pressed the back of his hand against the sting in his own nose. "I might as well join you. I've made no progress here."

Emma took the stairs and maneuvered through the hallway, and Liam kept close on her heels. Artie's bedroom was overflowing with clothing. Faded, patterned wallpaper peeled from the corners, and the blinds were dusty and uneven. Liam doubted the man had ever thrown anything away in his life.

Artie's bedside table was stacked with books, and he caught sight of a familiar title.

He displayed the cover with a grin. "He's got good taste in books."

A delightful wash of color spread across Emma's cheeks, and she ripped the book away. "No teasing."

The pages fanned, and a newspaper clipping fluttered to the stained carpet.

Grimacing, he retrieved the article. "It's an announcement for Ruth Garner's sixtieth birthday party." He flipped over the paper. "And an advertisement for hamburger night at the Eagle's Club."

"Ruth must be related to the sheriff."

"I'll ask him about it."

"I doubt it's important," she said. "Looks like Artie was using it as a bookmark. Probably just picked up the nearest thing. That's what I usually do."

He automatically reached to tuck the clipping into the breast pocket of his jacket before catching Emma's gaze. He wasn't wearing his jacket. Reading his intention, she laughed and took the paper from his fingers, then tucked it into the pocket.

She patted the spot. "There. Safe and sound."

An aching tightness squeezed his throat. He'd never asked for much in his life. Given how he'd grown up, he was grateful for a steady paycheck and a roof over his head. Everything else was God's bounty. The one time he'd prayed, for Jenny, his prayers had gone unanswered.

His needs were simple, but in that moment, he'd never wanted anything more in his life than to be the man he saw reflected in Emma's topaz eyes. Except he'd already told her too much. She was smart and curious. How much longer until she knew the whole truth about him? Before she turned away in disgust?

"What are you thinking?" she asked with a smile. "When you look at me like that."

He stood frozen by that smile, radiant and warm, the flash of brilliance that illuminated her vivid features. "I—"

Something whipped her attention toward the door. "Do you smell that?"

"Yes." Somehow managing to tear his gaze from her, he focused on the room once more. "That's smoke."

A seeping dread spread through his bloodstream.

"Something downstairs is burning," she gasped.

NINE

Emma clutched the back of Liam's shirt as he tested the knob before cracking open the door to the hallway. An aggressive plume of smoke billowed from the narrow opening. Slamming it shut, they stumbled away in unison.

Liam reached for the microphone attached to his collar, then paused and jabbed his finger toward a second door. "Wet some towels from the bathroom and shove them against heating vents."

She gave a brisk nod, attempting to project an air of unruffled confidence she didn't feel.

He rattled off the address into the microphone then said, "We've got a fire at the Druckerman place."

Alarm tangled inside her. She turned the spigots of Artie's rust-streaked porcelain sink and ran water over a pair of threadbare towels before stuffing them against the heating vents.

"Ten-four," came Rose's familiar voice. "Someone already called it in. Fire and rescue en route."

"Who? Who called it in?" Liam demanded.

"Bishop. He was swinging around again to see if Artie had shown up."

"Did he happen to mention that two people are trapped upstairs?"

"That's new information." Always the professional, Rose repeated the details before asking, "Who's trapped?"

"Emma and I."

"Fire and rescue en r-route," she repeated unsteadily. "I'm praying for you."

"Don't worry, Rose, I've been in worse jams."

Emma wanted to hijack his confidence for the coming ordeal. The muted roar and crackle of the fire rattled the windowpanes. The house was nothing but dry tinder, and the room was heating. As she stuffed more towels beneath the door, Liam struggled with the window.

"Stay back," he shouted. "It's painted shut."

He grasped a heavy lamp from the bedside table and shattered the glass, then leaned over the sill. Emma rushed to his side. There was at least a ten-foot drop to the sloped porch overhang, then another ten or more feet to the ground.

"It's too far," she groaned. "I can't jump that far."

Liam grasped her shoulders and turned her to face him. "We're not going to make it out through the front door. Redbird only has a volunteer fire department, and response time is too slow for this kind of aggressive fire."

The noises from the first floor were growing louder, and smoke seeped through the towels at the heating vents and billowed from the door hinges.

She coughed and nodded. "I understand."

Her pulse surged. He had enough to worry about without her panic. She wasn't exactly afraid of heights, but she didn't want to break an ankle, either.

He wrestled the mattress from the bed, and Emma took the other side without being told. He folded the unwieldy square in two and managed to shove it through the broken window. The edges stuck, and he grasped the window frame, leaning back as he kicked the bulky material. When the mattress broke free, he stumbled backward.

Emma stooped and measured the progress. It landed mostly on point, sliding a little to the left.

Liam blanched, and she followed his gaze. The wallpaper over the door to the hallway was peeling and drooping. Beads of sweat dripped from her temples, and Liam swiped the moisture covering his forehead. The space had turned into an oven in only a few minutes.

A crack sounded and she jumped, instinctively covering her ears.

Liam gently tugged her fingers free. "It's a ten-foot drop," he said, leaning forward, his voice calm. "I'll lower you as far as I can to mitigate the distance."

He draped a doubled-folded blanket over the broken window and beckoned for her. She shivered. Despite the rising temperature, her hands were slick with cold sweat and she rubbed them together.

As she threw one leg over the sill, she studied the distant horizon, hopelessly searching for help, her ears attuned for the comforting screech of sirens. Nothing. Which meant she had a choice. Stay or go. Deciding she'd much rather break a leg than burn to death, she took a shuddering breath.

She gave a hesitant nod. "Ready."

The room was blurring, the open window suctioning the suffocating clouds toward them. Liam pressed his watering eyes into the crook of his elbow and coughed.

She tipped farther over the ledge, and he grasped her arms.

"I'm going to lower you as far as I can," he said. "But you'll have to drop the rest of the distance."

Possibly she was more afraid of heights than she'd previously acknowledged. Numb with horror, she clutched his forearms and unfurled her legs from the safety of the windowsill. She'd read about people being petrified with fear, and now she understood the phrase. Her sneakers dangled, and she frantically scuffed at the siding. A sudden, overwhelming panic seized her.

"Emma!"

Liam was breathing rapidly from his exertions, and his face was set in grim lines. "You're going to have to let go."

The drop wasn't far with the deputy stretched as far as his arms would let him, but her fingers weren't cooperating.

"What about you?" she called.

"I'm right behind you."

He grimaced, and she recalled he'd been shot in the shoulder. The pain of supporting her must be excruciating.

She let go and her heart stopped dead. For a crystal moment time slowed, and the next instant she crashed to the mattress. Pain shot up her legs and her teeth clattered together so hard she was certain she'd chipped a molar. Collapsing to the side, she reached for the edge of the mattress and groped over the expanse of the porch roof. Liam was behind her, and she had to get out of his way.

She flashed him the thumbs up sign.

His back was barely visible as he crawled through the open window, his hands on the sill, his feet braced against the siding. His hold slipped, and he plummeted, landing hard. His left foot caught the mattress, but his right foot missed and slipped, yanking him over.

Clutching his shoulder, he staggered upright. "Ready to go again?"

Unable to force her legs to hold her upright, Emma crawled to the edge. An excruciating mix of alarm and fear rose through her limbs in hot panic. The drop was about the same distance as before. As she eyed the landing, Liam tossed the mattress to the ground below them.

Favoring his arm, he knelt beside her. "You got this. We'll do the same thing we did before."

He must have strained his shoulder lowering her, and he'd landed on the same side. There was no way she was letting him dangle her over the side and risk further injury. He needed that strength to save himself.

She grasped his cheeks and planted a hard kiss on his lips. "Be careful."

Without giving him a chance to react, she grasped the downspout and flipped herself over the side. The flimsy metal held for a glorious second before giving out beneath her weight. The break must have been enough to slow her fall, because the second landing wasn't as bad as the first.

She pushed herself upright and winced at the scrapes on her fingers.

Tenting her hand against the glare of the sun, she staggered backward, searching for Liam. He should have been right behind her.

She limped to the side, her arms outstretched as though she might somehow conjure him.

The next instant, her world exploded around her.

Liam stared at the vast expanse of the sky. There were clouds but no rain. Thunder but no lightning. His ears rang, but he couldn't remember where he was or how he'd gotten there. His whole body ached, though he didn't think anything was broken. Or maybe it was. He really didn't care right then.

He kept staring at the sky, hoping something would make sense soon.

Then his view went dim.

Someone was yelling at him, the words muffled against the ringing in his ears. The man's lips moved as he gestured frantically.

Liam flapped his good arm to keep the distraction at

bay. Maybe if he got a better look at the sky, he'd know what was going on.

He rolled his head to the side and studied the storm clouds. Only they weren't clouds at all. It was smoke. And the lightning wasn't lightning. Flames engulfed a white clapboard house, licking at the sky. Heat billowed over him in waves. The unmistakable scent of singed hair burned his nostrils.

The last few minutes came rushing back. The heat. The pain. The explosion.

"Emma!" he shouted, the word filtering through the ringing in his ears as a warbled mess. "Where is Emma?"

A hand looped beneath his shoulder, and he howled in pain, straining away. The man waved to someone out of Liam's vision.

Chad.

The man yelling at him was Chad. One of the volunteer firemen. Good. That was good. Someone had called dispatch. *He'd* called dispatch.

Chad switched sides. His mouth moved but no sounds reached Liam's ears. His world started to spin, and he closed his eyes against the throbbing agony in his shoulder.

He forced them open. Emma. He had to get to Emma.

A second man came into view. Bishop. The deputy hooked his arm beneath Liam's good shoulder and hauled him upright. The ground tilted and swayed. Bishop staggered. The deputy's spindly legs were barely enough to support his own weight, let alone Liam's.

There were flashing lights and sirens. The whole street was full of them. Every rescue vehicle in Redbird must be here.

Liam caught sight of Emma sitting on the tail end of the ambulance door with a silver blanket draped around her shoulders. He switched directions. Bishop seemed to be fighting the change of plans. Even disabled, Liam was stronger and more determined.

Bishop shouted something Liam couldn't hear.

His ears might be incapacitated, but there was nothing wrong with his eyes. She didn't appear injured. Her hair was tangled and disheveled, and there was a dark streak of soot across her face.

The silver blanket masked any other injuries she might have. She was sitting upright. That had to be a good sign.

Chad was hollering at him again, and the ringing had lessened enough Liam was able to make out a few words.

"The water heater blew," the young fireman yelled. "We thought we lost you. Must have knocked you back ten feet. I had to dig you out of the garden."

"Emma," he croaked.

"She's all right. You're not looking so good, though. You're gonna have to regrow that beard."

As Liam touched the singed remnants of his facial hair, the fireman chortled.

Liam's knees gave out. Emma tossed off the blanket and rushed toward him. His stomach heaved, and his vision collapsed around the edges until the light was only a pinprick.

Jenny's eyes swam before him.

Her hand was stretched toward him, palm up, and she touched his fingers. "Let them help you."

He frowned at her words. *Let who help him?*

Then she was gone, and Emma was in her place, her stunning topaz eyes shimmering with concern. "You're hurt. Let them help you."

"Are you all right?" he asked in a voice that didn't seem to belong to him.

"You've got a dislocated shoulder." Her breath puffed against his ear as she spoke. "Fortunately for you, I have some recent experience in this area. Unfortunately for you, I know what happens next. The fireman has to put it back in place."

Chad leaned over him, anchoring his helmet with one hand, the visor kicked back. "You're gonna be all right, but we gotta get this shoulder back in place." The young fireman grasped his wrist and braced his other hand against Liam's upper arm. "This is gonna hurt."

And just like that, the world went black.

Emma was immediately enchanted by the owner of the bed-and-breakfast where Liam was staying.

The older woman met them on the porch and ushered them inside. "I'm so glad the sheriff called. You poor things. I'm going to take care of you now. Don't you worry. We're gonna manage just fine."

Following the fire, Emma and Liam had spent the rest of the afternoon in the hospital emergency room. Both of them had refused to be admitted overnight. Since the doctor had seen no signs of a concussion, and the ringing in Liam's ears had abated, the medical staff had reluctantly agreed to release the deputy.

The sheriff had brought him a fresh uniform but otherwise he looked rather worse for wear. His beard and hair had been singed by the fire, though his eyebrows had mostly survived. Emma had fared far better. Her clothing smelled like smoke and she had a few scrapes and bruises along with a sore ankle, but that was the extent of her injuries.

Liam hung his hat on a peg by the door. "Blanche Slattery, meet Emma Lyons."

Blanche was slightly taller than Emma and reed thin. She wore a flowing tunic in muted shades of violet over deep purple leggings. Her hair was gunmetal gray with lighter streaks. She'd pulled the wavy mass from her temples and secured the strands with a beaded flower clip that matched her shirt.

"It's a pleasure," the older woman said. "Here's what we're going to do. The two of you are going to get cleaned up and have a rest. Are either of you hungry?"

They both groaned and shook off the idea of food. Emma touched her roiling stomach. She might have refused the hospital stay, but she wasn't fully recovered.

"All right," Blanche said with a frown. "But you're going to wake up famished, mark my words."

Even in her battered state, Emma appreciated her new environment. The enormous house was decorated to perfection. The furniture was Victorian-inspired in bold floral patterns. The ruby wallpaper gave the house an authentic feel without being fussy. Faded Oriental rugs in coordinating hues of navy and emerald were scattered over the polished oak floors, and a staircase with an ornate banister led to the second floor. Colorful light from a stained-glass transom window cast a pattern on the wall opposite the door.

Emma hesitated. "I hope you don't mind. I know you weren't expecting an extra guest."

After everything that had happened that day, she'd never made it home. When Liam mentioned staying with Blanche, she'd jumped at the chance. Even the idea of returning to her cold, empty house had sent shivers down her spine. There were people at the bed-and-breakfast, and light and warmth and a police officer parked outside, along with a deputy down the hall. Tomorrow was soon enough to go home.

"I run a hotel for all intents and purposes." Blanche leaned closer and pitched her voice to a loud whisper. "I'm always expecting guests." She crossed the room in three quick strides, her bangle bracelets clinking merrily together on her thin wrists. "C'mon. Follow me, Emma. I'll give you the nickel tour. This is the parlor, as you probably already guessed. Through those double doors is the library. The bookshelf on the west wall is the unofficial town lending library. Feel free to take a book or two before you leave. I need the shelf space. Every time someone has an estate sale around here, I manage to come home with a bag of books. I know I shouldn't, but I can't resist. Your room is upstairs."

She turned and grasped the banister, taking the stairs two at a time.

Exhaustion dragging her feet, Emma's toe caught the edge of a throw rug and she stumbled. Liam caught her against his side and steadied her. Their gazes clashed, and she swayed forward. He lifted his free hand and threaded his fingers through the hair at her temple. Warmth curled through her stomach.

She tweaked what was left of his beard. "Long day."

"Long day," he said, sighing.

"Are you going to rest?"

"I need to look up that case number Bishop mentioned." He stifled a yawn. "And maybe call in the ATF on the fire. Looks like arson. Probably attempted manslaughter, as well. Someone knew we were in that house."

Blanche leaned over the banister. "You're no good to anyone dead on your feet."

They exchanged a glance, and Emma scrunched her nose. "She's right, you know."

Together they trudged up the stairs. Liam took a left, and Emma followed Blanche to the right. Her overnight bag was already sitting in the room Blanche had chosen for her, and she didn't bother asking how it had gotten there. After a bracing shower, she collapsed facedown onto the quilted comforter where she spent the next eight hours in blissful oblivion.

By the time light filtered through the blinds once more, she was feeling almost human again. Another shower finally removed the sooty tar from her hair, and she descended the stairs, following the delightful aroma of fresh-brewed coffee.

As she passed the dining room, Emma did a double take. "I hardly recognize you."

Liam had shaved his beard, revealing a strong, square jaw and high cheekbones. His hair was slicked back and neat. He was handsome before. Without the beard, he was devastating. She must have been staring because his expression grew confused.

"What's the matter? Did I miss a spot?" he asked.

"No," she said, her throat dry. "You look great."

He absently scratched at a razor nick on his neck. "You sure it's all right?"

"Fine," she croaked.

"I was just checking on Duchess," he said, leaning down. "Hang in there, little lady We'll take good care of you."

Catching a glimpse of a wagging tail, Emma quirked an eyebrow. "That's the dog you think might belong to Artie?"

He straightened, and when he discovered Emma studying him, flushed and rubbed a hand down his smooth chin. For such a handsome man, he appeared unaccustomed to attention. His awkwardness was both endearing and charming.

"Yep," he said. "My unofficial deputy. Mrs. Slattery has been watching her while I'm at work." The tips of his ears darkened to a rosy hue. "Turns out Duchess is expecting any day now. With everything else happening, I failed to notice she was in a, uh, in the family way."

"I'm sure she's forgiven you." Emma tiptoed past the room and whispered, "What are you going to do with the puppies?"

"That's the thing. I don't know. If we don't hear from Artie soon…"

"Do you think he's…"

"I don't know what to think." Liam rushed to reassure her. "We're pulling everyone in on this one. If he's out there, we'll find him."

"I hope he's all right."

"You and I have other things to worry about. Like breakfast. Mrs. Slattery was right. I'm famished."

"Told you so," a voice called from the kitchen.

Emma and Liam giggled like a couple of kids caught with their hands in the cookie jar. Taking an hour for breakfast wasn't going to change anything. Right now, she was in a beautiful home with mouthwatering aromas wafting from the kitchen. The company was good, and the outside world was far away. She simply wanted to enjoy the here and now.

The pictures lining the hallway were a hodgepodge of frames depicting various eras in time in no particular order. The eclectic mishmash was charming, and Emma paused before the stoic face of a handsome marine.

Liam leaned down and spoke close to her ear. "That's Mrs. Slattery's son, Ben." His breath whispered against her skin, sending gooseflesh pebbling down her arm. "He was killed in Afghanistan ten years ago."

"How sad."

Emma noted several more pictures of Ben throughout his short life. He was a handsome, serious young man with kind eyes that reminded her of his mother's. A man she assumed was Ben's father was featured in a few of the earlier pictures, but the latter were only of Ben and Blanche.

"How long have you been staying here?" she asked, hoping to turn the subject to something lighter.

"About six months."

She quirked an eyebrow. "Having problems finding a place of your own?"

"Something like that." He scratched his temple. "It's a long story."

"I'm a good listener."

Her curiosity was an asset to an investigative journalist but a liability in personal relationships, as Jordan often chastised her.

"I imagine I've overstayed my welcome," he said. "Even as a paying customer."

Was his "unfinished business" the reason he was reluctant to put down roots? If so, what was he waiting for? Why didn't he leave immediately? As her interest took flight, she stifled a groan. The slices of her personality that made her good at investigative journalism didn't help much in social situations.

Her books and articles had been described as in-depth character studies. She wanted to understand what drove people to behave as they did. She always read the last page of a mystery first, because the "what" was just as important as the "why." Human beings were naturally creatures of habit, and serial killers were often caught when behavioral profilers unraveled their patterns and pieced together the clues.

The Lonestar State Killer had been different. He often favored the same gun, but the shootings were almost an afterthought. He hunted in different neighborhoods, and they'd yet to discover a link between the victims. More than once there'd been reports of a Peeping Tom in the neighborhood before he struck, but just as often, the murders had been shockingly random.

The arbitrary use of the gun had always troubled her. Why bother to link himself to his victims in such a clumsy manner? There must be a reason, and the "what" was as important as the "why."

If the Lonestar Killer was the person stalking her, and if he thought she'd discovered a clue to his identity, why hadn't he killed her already? He'd obviously been watching her. She'd been alone when she left the house that night. Why hadn't he silenced her when he had the opportunity?

If he'd set fire to the house, had he been watching their escape?

As they entered the kitchen, Blanche turned, her tiny hands dwarfed by enormous floral-patterned oven mitts. She wore another diaphanous purple shirt with flowing sleeves.

"Liam." She gestured with her mitts. "Can you finish setting the table?"

"Sure thing."

Through the clatter of silverware and dishes, the two worked well together. Blanche treated Liam with the affection of a favored child, and he deferred to her with the same caring respect. They laughed and joked, although Liam appeared to be holding a part of himself in check. There was a guarded quality to his answers and a hesitancy in his speech. Emma doubted he was even aware of his actions. If Blanche noticed, she didn't let on.

One thing was certain—if Liam thought he was overstaying his welcome, he was sorely mistaken. Blanche clearly doted on him.

When the table settings were finally in place, the three of them took their chairs around the square table. Blanche realized she had forgotten the butter and started to rise. Liam waved her back to her seat and retrieved the dish himself. If Emma wasn't already starting to fall for him, the considerate gesture would have pushed her over the edge.

Much to her relief, the older woman dominated the conversation throughout the meal, chatting about local gossip and the weather.

They avoided the topic as long as they could before Blanche finally brought up the subject. "I was sorry to hear about Artie's place. He's going to be devastated. That house belonged to his parents and his grandparents before that. I don't know him well, mind you, but in a small town, everyone knows everyone else to some degree. We're both members of the Redbird Historical Society. It's not really a society so much as an excuse to gossip. But there you have it."

Liam topped off his coffee from the carafe on the table. "We heard he was digitizing the Redbird *Gazette*. Did he talk about that much?"

"Ad nauseum," Blanche muttered with a sardonic grin. "Artie loves to spin a tale and reading through the past twenty years of Redbird news was absolute nirvana."

"Then he liked to keep up with the local rumor mill," Liam said thoughtfully.

"Considered himself the keeper of town lore. Not that there was much lore to keep. There isn't much crime around here."

"There was a murder, though." Emma said. "That must have been memorable."

"You don't know the half of it," Blanche declared in a conspiratorial whisper. "Really shook up this town.'

Emma leaned forward. "Then you knew Missy Johnson."

There was no better source than a local to know all the details that failed to make the front page.

"Odd that you should mention both Missy and Artie in the same conversation," Blanche replied. "I hadn't thought about her in years until Artie asked me about the murder just the other day."

Emma and Liam exchanged a look, and her heart pounded against her ribs. There was no way Artie's curiosity was a coincidence.

TEN

Mrs. Slattery's declaration snagged Liam's attention.

He'd initially been skeptical that a twenty-year-old murder case with a cut and dried conviction had anything to do with Emma's stalker. As the coincidences added up, his conviction was faltering.

"Artie said he might have some information about the case," Liam said casually. "You don't happen to know if he discovered anything new?"

"No. Mostly he wanted to pick my brain about what I remembered from that time. I figured he wanted to write a book or something. I could see Artie wanting to write about Redbird. We were going to talk more but haven't found a time to get together yet."

"What did you tell him?" Liam asked, curious about the same thing.

"I know it sounds like a cliché." Mrs. Slattery stared into space. "But I remember it like it was yesterday. My son, Ben, was still at home, and my husband traveled quite a bit at the time. We were fixing up this house, and I'd hear every little creak and groan when he was gone. Used to get myself all kinds of worked up." She gave a nervous chuckle. "Still do, sometimes. Ben's dad died in a car accident outside Colleyville some years back. Although, since Liam's been here, I'm not nearly as jumpy. There's nothing like having a big, strong deputy in the house to make an old lady feel safe."

Liam frowned. "You're not an old lady."

"And you're a terrible liar. Anyway, about Missy Johnson. She was dating Deputy Bishop's younger brother. Everyone was expecting an engagement. She'd been missing a few days when some folks on vacation found the body on the shore of the lake. I didn't know Missy well, mind you. She ran with a younger crowd, and I was a married lady with a child to raise by then. I knew her mother a little better. Went to church together, though the Johnsons mostly kept to themselves. The family moved away after Missy died."

The fine hairs on the nape of Liam's neck stirred. "Deputy Bishop knew the murder victim?"

"Everyone knew Missy. The town was even smaller back then."

Gossip in a small town spread like wildfire. If someone was asking questions, how long before that information got back to a person who had a stake in the outcome? Especially if a bestselling writer from Dallas was asking the questions.

"Did Artie talk about the man who murdered Missy?" Emma asked.

"A drifter confessed." The corners of Mrs. Slattery's mouth turned down. "Of course, he died in prison proclaiming his innocence. Said they coerced him into the confession. But killers never take responsibility, do they? I don't mean to sound dramatic, but it felt like the murder changed the whole town. As though we all lost our innocence."

"How do you mean?"

"Murder and crime were problems for big city folks. But that simply isn't so, is it? We were naive, and Missy paid the price. We had a different sheriff back then. What was his name..." She snapped her fingers. "Phillips. That was his name. Sheriff Phillips. He was a nice man, mind you, but he was in a rush to solve the case before the tourist season started. Wouldn't want all those folks from Dallas to stop spending their money in town because there was a murderer on the loose."

Liam hadn't heard the name before. "Does Phillips still live around here?"

"No. He died some years back. That was when Sheriff Garner ran for office. He'd recently retired from the Fort Worth Police Department and was doing some contract work with the county. Delivering court summons when the department was backed up. That sort of thing."

A familiar swell of emotion spiked through Liam. All cases were, at their heart, a riddle waiting to be solved. No one stayed invisible in a small town, which meant that relationships were often intertwined and complicated. Cold cases were even more challenging, especially when the witnesses were deceased. Speaking with the source was always better than reading old case notes.

"Funny how things work out," Mrs. Slattery said. "Bishop was interim sheriff after the car accident, and he figured he was a sure thing to win the special election. He hadn't counted on Garner running. I think it stuck in his craw. That's why he throws his name into the election every four years. He'll never win, though. Not in this county. People know who they like."

"I didn't realize the sheriff was from Redbird," Liam said, reaching for another slice of toast out of the basket. "I thought he was from Fort Worth."

The realization left him oddly unsettled. He'd assumed they were both transplants, considering the sheriff's job history, though the topic hadn't exactly come up in conversation.

"Born and raised here." Mrs. Slattery settled back in her chair and spread her arms, her sheer lavender sleeves draping like delicate bird wings. "Poor Sheriff Garner. Now there's a man who's had more than his fair share of tragedy. His first wife ran off on him. I think that's why he moved to Fort Worth in the first place. Too many painful memories."

"His first wife?" Emma raised her voice at the end of the sentence in question.

"Yes. After his wife deserted him, he remarried. But he's been widowed now. Although I heard he's been seen out and about with one of the tellers from the bank. He's a good catch. Surprised someone hasn't snatched him up by now."

Liam grinned. "Ever thought about casting a line for him yourself?"

"Not me." Blanche's look of horror was comical. "I like my freedom."

At least the sheriff's history with his first wife explained why he'd never mentioned his connection to the town. No one wanted that kind of gossip stirred up.

Understanding how the town worked was key to solving local investigations. Many of the people who lived in Redbird around the time of Missy's death might still be living here. Emma's memories around the previous week were fuzzy, leaving them handicapped. Who else had she talked with concerning the murder?

He circled back to how the conversation had started. "But Artie didn't mention anything specific? He didn't have any suspicions about the case?"

"Not that I know of." Blanche considered the question. "Must get boring scanning page after page after page. That's probably what got him talking about Missy. That case dominated the headlines around here for weeks. Artie is nearly sixty, and he's not a bit intimidated by those computers. I can hardly use a phone these days. If you want to know something about the history of Redbird, Artie is the one you'd ask."

Liam had been in law enforcement long enough to know that a conviction didn't always end a case. What if Emma had stumbled onto a local mystery someone wanted to keep buried? How close had she come to exposing the truth?

Time had a way of loosening people's tongues. Relationships often broke down over the years, severing old alliances. Sometimes people simply tired of carrying the burden of a secret. Someone who may have clammed up twenty years ago might be itching to set the record straight.

Bishop's brother had been dating the victim, and Emma wanted to speak with the local historian about the murder. That kept things interesting. Too bad the sheriff wasn't living in town around that time. Garner had a mind like a steel trap.

Emma seemed to be concentrating, absorbing the information with equal focus. "You should be the town historian, Blanche, you know everyone."

"Not everyone. But you stick around one place long enough, you get to know people. That's what I like about living in Redbird. I never feel like I'm alone. I'm always running into someone I know. Mind you, not everyone likes that part of living in a small town." She cast a withering glance in Liam's direction. "But you're getting used to it, aren't you?"

"I am," he reluctantly conceded. "I'm even starting to like the old place."

"It grows on you," she said.

"Like a wart," he joked.

The three of them laughed. Leave it to Mrs. Slattery to bring that up. For a guy accustomed to living in the shadows, the first few weeks in town had been a shock. As the days had turned into months, he'd come to see the benefits.

There were situations where familiarity was an asset. Vice cops tended to be battering rams rather than peacemakers. His time in Redbird had revealed a skill set he hadn't known he possessed. Most of his current job revolved around helping people, and he hadn't expected the satisfaction that came from that sort of work.

Though initially frustrated by the petty disputes of fences encroaching on property lines and phantom prowlers, he'd come to recognize the complex issues simmering beneath the surface. He had a previously untapped instinct for mediation. Disputes were often a symptom of a deeper problem, and he was learning to dig beneath the surface for the root of the animosity.

Six months ago, he'd never have believed he'd be interested in the inner workings and history of a small town in Texas, but he was fascinated by the lesson. Emma appeared equally enthralled.

"Hard to believe we were all young once, isn't it?" Mrs. Slattery shook her head. "Some days I feel like I'm still in my thirties, and some days I feel like I've been old forever. I knew Sheriff Garner's mother, Ruth. Salt of the earth, that woman. That's why I always remember the day of Missy's murder. It was Ruth's sixtieth birthday. The sheriff's older brother organized the party."

"Sheriff Garner has an older brother?"

"Yes. The brothers didn't get along. The sheriff didn't even come to the party. Good thing, too. Those two were likely to brawl. Although I haven't seen the brother in years. I think he moved to Tampa. Anyway, I was sorry when Ruth passed, but I'm glad Sheriff Garner came home. He took real good care of her before she died."

Blanche stood and opened a cupboard, then frowned. "Now that's odd. Liam, did you move the sugar bowl?"

"Nope."

"Humph." She shrugged and started to close the cupboard door, then paused. "Here it is. Never mind. I must have moved it and forgot. Been doing that a lot lately. Getting old isn't for sissies."

Liam added more names to his list of suspects. In Bishop's last bid for the sheriff's office, he'd bragged about being on the force for over twenty years. How involved had he been in Missy's murder investigation? That must have been sticky, considering his brother's involvement with the victim. The sheriff's brother had been in town, as well. Any one of them might have a reason to hide evidence, but only Bishop had the opportunity.

Emma seemed to be processing the information, as well. She studied her plate, her brow furrowed, her index finger tapping against the table.

"What about Deputy Bishop's brother?" Liam asked. "The one who was dating Missy. What happened to him?"

Boyfriends and family members were always the first suspects. There must have been a reason Bishop's brother was eliminated, which should be noted in the case file. Except small towns weren't always known for meticulous record keeping. And there was always the chance someone close to the case had gotten to the files first.

"Grant Bishop moved back to town about the same time as the sheriff did. He and his wife run an antiques shop in the town square. Their prices are too high, if you ask me, but Grant has a good eye for furniture."

The rush of starting a new case got Liam's blood pumping. The first chance he got, he vowed to piece together a time line of the killing along with the people involved. He'd also need more information on Bishop's brother. He'd check and see if Grant had shown up on any law enforcement radars over the years. He'd track down the sheriff's brother while he was at it.

Who knew what sorts of jealousies were simmering beneath the surface all those years ago?

"For such a small town," Emma said, "Redbird has its share of drama."

"I think most towns are like that," Mrs. Slattery said. "Doesn't matter how small. You put three people together, and there's bound to be trouble sooner or later. That's the nature of man."

On the surface, Redbird seemed like a run-of-the-mill community with a church on every corner and a smile on every face. It didn't take too much digging to come up with secrets and lies.

Mrs. Slattery stood and turned toward the sink. "Anyone want any coffee?"

"I'll take some," Liam said. "Thank you."

He'd taken some aspirin for his bumps and bruises, but he'd spent a restless night tossing and turning. The few times he'd dozed off, he'd rolled onto his sore arm and woken himself up again.

"None for me." Emma rested her chin on her palm. "Do you think there's any evidence left from the case?"

Liam ran his hand down his face. He hadn't been able to gauge her reaction this morning. She'd seemed tongue-tied, and he didn't know if that was a good or a bad sign. As a teenager, he'd done his fair share of primping in front of a mirror. As an adult, he hadn't given much thought to his looks. He chose his clothes and his facial hair to blend in. Glancing down, he brushed the front of his shirt. He'd been wearing basically the same thing for the past week. Maybe it was time to shake it up.

"The case," Emma prodded, her expression telling him

she'd asked more than once while he pondered his lack of wardrobe. "Do you have access to the old case files?"

"There should be something in storage." He had a bad feeling they were going to come up empty. From what he'd seen over the past six months, file storage wasn't a priority for the county sheriff's office. "I'll ask Rose to pull the files."

DNA evidence had overturned plenty of murders in recent years. There was always a chance the man convicted of killing Missy was telling the truth about his innocence. Either way, the case was worth a second look. Especially with Bishop's family showing up in the mix.

His phone buzzed, and he glanced at the number.

Time slowed, and he fought to calm his pulse and keep his expression neutral.

The US Marshals were making contact.

The next instant, his temper flared. After six months of letting him dangle in the wind with no information, he was supposed to drop everything and do their bidding. He had a case; he had responsibilities. How was he going to explain his absence to Emma? Who did he trust to follow up the case?

The irony was that six days ago, he'd have leaped at the chance to leave and never looked back.

Turned out, dying was easy. Staying dead was the hard part.

With her memory almost fully intact, the business of living took precedence. Emma discovered that near-fatal car accidents were expensive and filled with paperwork.

Feeling lost without her electronic devices, she'd ordered a new laptop and she and Liam had replaced her phone. The moment the young polo-clad clerk at the store had connected her account with her new phone, a series of text messages had scrolled down the screen to a slot-machine cacophony of notifications.

For over an hour she'd painstakingly replied to messages, calling the most frantic friends and apologizing for her slow response to others. With the people she phoned, she'd downplayed the seriousness of the accident, mentioning only that she'd had to replace her electronics.

Explaining the same story over and over again while assuring people she was healthy and fine had left her oddly exhausted.

"Life is far less complicated when you don't remember anything." She laughed. "I have nearly two hundred emails to sort through."

When she could no longer avoid the inevitable, she directed Liam to take her home. If he thought her reluctance odd, he kept his own counsel. Since seeing the pictures her attacker had taken of her leaving her house, she'd been reluctant to return alone. The place that should have been her haven no longer felt safe.

Liam parked his SUV on a tree-lined boulevard and gestured. "Here we are."

Angling her head, she studied the two-story Victorian with a wraparound porch and cupola.

She'd seen the property for sale online and had been drawn to the pictures immediately. The Realtor had done his best to show the house at an advantage, downplaying the peeling wallpaper and the stained linoleum in the kitchen. None of that had mattered. She'd done her research on the town. After a weekend visit, she'd decided to proceed.

Her stepbrother had advised her against the purchase. He'd said the house was a money pit, and that she didn't know anything about home renovation. He was right. She'd ordered an inspection anyway. The house had "solid

bones," the inspector had said, and the difficulties between her and Jordan had started long before she'd purchased the house anyway.

She glanced around, hardly aware she was approaching
the front door until Liam called for her to wait.

He retrieved his phone from his pocket and glanced at
the screen. Something in his expression told her the call
was important.

"I have to take this," he said.

"Is everything all right?"

"Yeah. Fine." He held the phone to his ear and gestured. "This shouldn't take long. Don't go inside without
me. I want to check out the house first."

"Okay."

He turned and strode a few paces down the sidewalk,
his body language tense. She circled around the house and
tested the locked back door to give him some privacy. Despite his protests, she sensed he was upset about the call.

After making her way to the front of the house once
more, she took the shallow porch stairs and tented her
hand against the window, unable to see through the shuttered blinds. Pacing the distance, she caught sight of Liam,
his back turned, one hand braced against the hood of his
police vehicle.

On impulse, she retrieved her keys from her pocket.
While she appreciated his caution, she doubted there was
any need to worry.

She let herself inside and paused just over the thresh-
old. Her hand automatically pressed against the light
switch. There was no furniture in the front room, which
left the partially stripped wood floors exposed. An elec-
tric sander, rags and a gallon of floor stain were neatly
stacked in the corner. The can had been left open, stinging
her nose with a pungent, chemical smell. She knew with-

out a shadow of doubt that she'd never be that careless. Not to mention the house was freezing. The ancient thermostat on the wall just inside the entry was set to sixty degrees, the lowest the dial could be set. Another oddity.

She shivered and rubbed her upper arms. The living room was overflowing with boxes and books, forming a short wall before the exposed brick fireplace. The kitchen was situated near the back of the house, down a hallway.

Moving to the right, she entered the living room.

Her pulse jerked. This was wrong. This was all wrong. The house was a disaster.

She knelt and grasped a crumpled paper. Someone had ripped open every single box in the room and scattered the contents over the floor. She stared blankly at the disorder.

Her whole body trembled. He'd been here. She was certain this was the work of her stalker. He'd rifled through her belongings.

Slowly maneuvering around the debris, she made her way to the parlor. She planned on turning the space into her office and had already positioned her desk before the enormous windows looking out over the front lawn.

A man's shoe rested on the floor. She took a cautious step forward. There was no reason for a man's shoe to be in her house.

Scooting around the desk, she glanced down.

Her mind went blank, and for a moment she couldn't make sense of what she was seeing. Gasping, she backed away. Her world went dark around the edges, and she swayed.

An older, heavyset man lay sprawled on the floor between the stack of boxes and the empty fireplace. He appeared to be in his late sixties or early seventies, with wispy gray hair. His pale gray eyes stared unseeing at the ceiling.

Liam's footsteps approached and his voice sounded behind her. "Why is it so cold in here—" He broke off, his attention snagged by the body. "Don't touch anything."

"I haven't." She gestured vaguely. "The light switch. That was all."

"Are you all right?" His hands closed over her shoulders. "You're shivering. Do you want to step outside? A lot of people are distraught by seeing a dead body. Don't feel bad."

"I'm fine." Her nerves were electrified, and her focus sharpened. She took in the layout of the room and the placement of the body. "The living are far more frightening to me than the dead."

She had a knack for analyzing crime scenes. She'd spent years of her life staring at the photos and looking for clues, although nothing had prepared her for the real thing. Swallowing back the bile churning in her stomach, she forced herself to analyze the details.

"He was lured here," she said.

Discovering the surveillance photos of herself had nearly broken her. This was different. Murder was her life's work. She was far more comfortable with analysis than she was with being a victim—even if the man's unseeing eyes did give her the chills.

"I don't follow." Liam's expression was quizzical.

"The doors were locked. I checked just now. He's not a small man and he's no spring chicken. He didn't shimmy in through a window. He was invited in."

She took a halting step forward.

Liam held up a restraining hand. "Hang on a second." He snagged a wad of surgical gloves from the pouch at his waist. "Put these on, just in case."

She expertly donned the gloves, her muscle memory performing the act with neat precision. She'd handled evidence from cases in the past, though never this immediately. All those hours of piecing together the last moment of a victim's life had given her certain insights and instincts.

"The killer was probably standing a little to your right," she said. "Where he wouldn't be visible from the door. The victim walked in and was struck from behind." Monitoring her breathing to keep calm, she examined the ceiling. "There's blood spatter from the blow. No obvious sign of a murder weapon. The victim never saw what hit him. He may not have died right away, but he never regained consciousness. There's no blood smears around the body."

Liam knelt and examined the area. "He's not in rigor mortis. That means he's been dead no longer than twelve, maybe twenty-four hours."

"Who is it? Do you recognize him?"

"No. Let's take a look."

A second later Liam straightened, a leather wallet in his hands.

He retrieved the man's identification, and his eyes widened. "Artie Druckerman."

"Artie?" Unable to move the body without disturbing the evidence, she circled around for a better look at his face. "The poor man."

"If only we could tell how long he's been here."

"The killer wanted the house cold to preserve the body. There's an open can of floor stripper. He didn't want the neighbors..."

"Noticing the smell." Liam gave a curt nod, and she sensed his admiration. "Anything to buy more time."

"He didn't think I was coming home anytime soon."

"My thoughts exactly. Stay here. For real, this time. I doubt the killer is still in the house, but I have to check."

Bouncing on the balls of her feet, she waited impatiently for his return.

His footsteps sounded on the second floor, and a few

minutes later he reappeared again. "It's clear. The sheriff isn't going to be happy with this turn of events."

He made the necessary calls, rattling off the pertinent details of the crime scene.

Liam stowed his phone and glanced around the room. "We don't have much time. In a few minutes, this place is going to be overrun by the Redbird police. There's the chief, the sergeant and four officers. My guess, they're all going to show up to get a gander at a murder scene. If we're going to save any evidence, we have to work fast. Whoever murdered Artie was looking for something. If we know what that is, it will help the investigation. Do you have a computer? A laptop or a tablet or something?"

She snapped her fingers. "Yes! On the desk."

He circled around the body and searched. "There's nothing here. I checked around the rest of the house and didn't see anything. We have to get you out of here before the evidence team arrives. Take a good look now. See if there's anything else missing."

"There are files missing." She pointed to an open shelf. "There were books and files on that shelf, and they're all gone."

"Are you certain?"

"Yes."

"What was in them?"

"Notes on my current book. Things like that."

A shadow flitted across his face. "All right. That's better than nothing." He took her arm and guided her toward the door. "I can't stay with you once the police arrive. I won't be able to talk to you. Do you have a lawyer?"

"A lawyer," she said in a strangled whisper. "Why would I need a lawyer?"

Sirens sounded in the distance, and he maneuvered them toward the door. "That's the Redbird police. Think how this looks, Emma. This guy was in your house. You don't remember what happened last week."

Car doors slammed, and voices sounded outside.

"Wait a second." She whirled around with a gasp. "What are you saying?"

"At the very least, the Redbird police are going to bring you in for questioning. I'll advocate for you, I promise. I can vouch for your whereabouts since the car accident. But we can't avoid reality. There's a very real chance you're going to be a suspect in Artie's murder."

Her knees turned to jelly. "A suspect?"

ELEVEN

Liam paced the dismal waiting room of the Redbird Police Department, only half listening to the chatter of the officers on duty. They hadn't arrested Emma yet, but they'd been questioning her for the past hour.

His hand spasmed, spilling the cup of coffee he clutched. He dumped the contents in the trash and shook out his wrist. He'd finally gotten assistance with the case, though not exactly as planned. With Artie's murder, jurisdiction extended to the Redbird police. They had more manpower. They also had Emma at the station for questioning.

Frustrated, he studied a rust-colored stain on the ancient ceiling tiles. The one constant in his life had always been bad timing.

The phone call from the US Marshals had left his head spinning, and he hadn't had time to sort the details. They were summoning him back to Dallas when Emma needed him most. He'd argued. They'd threatened. According to the Marshals, they'd created his deputy persona as a cover until the trial, and that day had arrived. They weren't interested in subsidizing his continued involvement in a small-town investigation that held no interest to them.

Failure to answer the summons meant possible criminal charges. He was looking at a week or more of behind-closed-doors testimony that didn't exactly allow time for a lengthy commute.

The outside door swung open with a noticeable amount

of force, snagging Liam's attention. A man in a dark suit strode into the building. The wind flipped his jacket aside, revealing a sidearm.

Liam stood.

The man crossed the distance to the counter, and a wet-behind-the-ears officer planted his bulky weight in the man's path.

"I'm sorry, sir. You'll have to step back."

The man held up his hands, his expression annoyed, his voice calm. "I'm Jordan Harris with the Department of Defense. I'm reaching for my identification."

Liam hoisted an eyebrow. Jordan was someone accustomed to giving orders. Accustomed to being in charge.

The officer said something, and Jordan's voice ticked up a notch. "Then I want to see the chief."

The officer ordered him to wait and disappeared down the corridor. A second policeman stepped forward and took his position, eyeing the newcomer with suspicion.

Making a decision, Liam crossed the distance and stuck out his hand. "Deputy Liam McCourt. I heard you say your name before. You're Jordan Harris, right?"

"Right." Emma's stepbrother gave his hand a brief, perfunctory shake. "You don't look like the man in charge here. I need to talk to the chief."

Liam squashed his flare of annoyance. Jordan Harris had clearly been traveling all night. His dark suit was heavily creased where he'd been sitting, and he'd removed his sunglasses, revealing deep lines beneath his eyes.

"The chief doesn't seem to be in a hurry to talk to you," Liam said with a glance in the officer's direction. "You have questions, and I have answers. Why don't we talk outside?"

Jordan muttered something beneath his breath. "Fine."

As the door closed behind them, Liam crossed his arms over his chest. "You're here about Emma Lyons, aren't you?"

"Look, I don't have time for this." Jordan speared his hands through his dark, neatly clipped hair. "I've spent the past forty-eight hours on a series of transport planes from the Middle East. Not exactly the most comfortable way to travel. I finally get to Redbird, and my sister's house is covered in police tape. What is going on?"

"She's all right. Don't worry," Liam quickly assured him. "Maybe it's best I start from the beginning."

Liam quickly relayed the events leading up to the discovery of Artie Druckerman's body, and Jordan sank weakly onto the bench set before the police station.

He clasped his hands before him and hung his head. "You're saying she doesn't remember the week leading up to the accident?"

"No. She has a flash of memory concerning the accident, but that's it."

"She needs a lawyer. They're going to chew her up and spit her out."

Liam had urged her to remain silent and call a lawyer. That was over an hour ago. His hands were tied.

The heavyset officer leaned out the door. "The chief says it'll be about another ten minutes."

Liam propped his hands on his utility belt. "You filing an arrest warrant?"

"That's above my pay grade. The chief said ten minutes. Now I'm telling you."

Once he'd gone, Jordan grunted. "Everyone in town like that?"

"Go easy on him. This is the most excitement they've had since Joe Keyes shot up his truck with a double-barrel shotgun because the engine died."

Jordan's posture changed, and his hazel eyes grew watchful. "What's your story?"

"No story," Liam said loudly, more forcefully than he'd intended. "I'm just a small-town deputy."

"I don't think so. Why all this interest in my sister?"

Emma was his stepsister, but Liam didn't correct him. "Just doing my job."

"I think there's more to you than meets the eye." Jordan stood and turned toward the door. "I have sources. If you're hiding something, I'll find out. I won't risk Emma's safety."

Liam kept his face carefully composed. He doubted even Jordan could discover his true identity, but his manufactured past wasn't going to satisfy the man for long. *Timing.* Looked like his timing wasn't going to improve anytime soon.

"If you have sources," Liam said, "then don't waste them on me. Use them to keep your sister out of jail. I saw the damage done to Artie. She's not capable of doing that. We don't know if we're dealing with a serial killer, a drug dealer, or some local with a secret worth killing to keep. All we know is that she's in danger."

Jordan seemed to be waging some sort of internal battle before he finally spoke. "Fine. I want all the evidence you have. The DNA. Everything."

Liam regarded the man with frank sympathy. Jordan was frustrated. He'd been dropped into a situation that was fraught with unknowns. He was clearly a man accustomed to commanding attention, and he'd been forced to cool his heels.

"Did you hear me?" Jordan inquired acidly. "I want everything."

A humorless smile pulled at Liam's lips. "We've already run the DNA through the system."

"Not my system. The Department of Defense has certain privileges that aren't available to Texas law enforcement."

"Point taken," Liam said equably. There was no harm

in taking a second look. "If you clear the jurisdiction, I'll get you everything I have."

"Thanks," the other man grudgingly conceded. "I'll get jurisdiction. I have contacts."

Liam might be angrier if he didn't understand what the man was going through. He was worried about Emma, and he was helpless. After spending the past hour grappling with the same feelings, there was little point in getting his back up over Jordan's rudeness.

"The deeper this case goes," Liam said, "the more I'm convinced this has something to do with Missy Johnson's murder."

A haunted look skittered over Jordan's face. "That was a long time ago." He chafed his hands over his pant legs. His unease was a chink in his armor. "We were kids."

"Emma said your dad claimed he discovered the body. Someone in this town is on edge. Harris is a common surname, but with all the dust getting stirred up these days, you can't be too careful."

Jordan sent him a simmering glare. "I can take care of myself."

Liam wrestled back his flare of annoyance once more. "Friendly warning. Nothing more."

"I'll keep that in mind." Jordan stood and shook out his arms, then rolled his neck. "That's ten minutes."

Liam followed him into the police station and froze.

Emma was standing a few feet away, her face pale.

Jordan stopped short. Emma staggered, her knees buckling. Liam started forward. Her stepbrother was closer. Jordan caught her and guided her to a lobby chair. The officers milling around the station parted for them, both curious and detached at the same time. As though recognizing they were unwanted bystanders.

Emma collapsed onto a seat and shocked them both

by bursting into tears. Her hands jerked up to her face, and sparkling rivulets seeped from between her fingers.

"You came," she managed to say through a muffled sob. "I asked them to tell you not to come."

"Absolutely I came," Jordan said, his voice heavy with emotion. "You were hurt. Where else would I be?"

"I don't even know where to start. There was an accident. Now there's been a murder."

"I know." Jordan scooped her into his embrace. "It's all right. We'll talk about everything later. Catch your breath."

"I d-don't know why I'm c-crying." She hiccuped into his shoulder. "It's like that blow to my head shook all my emotions loose. I can't seem to control them anymore."

"Then don't try."

Liam hovered helplessly, feeling like an intruder and hesitating to leave. His jealousy made absolutely no sense. This was Emma's brother. He had every right to hold and comfort her. Liam, on the other hand, had no rights. He was days away from doing the one thing he feared—abandoning her. He'd known when he took the case he might be called back, and he'd forged ahead anyway. Jordan's arrival was ideal under the circumstances.

It just felt rotten.

The Redbird police chief was a short, wiry man about Sheriff Garner's age, with a prominent gap between his teeth. Squirming beneath Jordan's piercing gaze, the chief quickly explained that they weren't arresting Emma, but they didn't want her to leave town, either. With an admiring look at Jordan's credentials, the chief promised to keep them updated on any new developments in the case.

Jordan searched the room for Liam. "I can't take her back to her house. Not after what happened. Where's the nearest hotel?"

"I'll do you one better."

Jordan must have been expecting an argument, because he visibly relaxed when Liam readily agreed. The two exchanged phone numbers, and Liam texted him Mrs. Slattery's address.

Emma huddled beside her stepbrother, pale and ghost-like.

She caught Liam staring and flashed a wan smile. "I'm fine, really."

He didn't have much time left. Monday was only a few days away.

Sirens sounded in the distance, and he was drawn to the past once more. Barely conscious during the ambulance ride that fateful night, he'd felt his life draining away with his blood. That same feeling struck him now. His future was slipping away with each passing hour.

The realization brought on a familiar panic—the need to sort out his unfinished business before time was snatched away from him. When he left, he needed to know that Emma was safe. He owed her that much, at least.

An elusive memory tugged at him. He texted Rose and asked her for the name on the case file Bishop had mentioned to Emma.

The reply came almost immediately, and his ears buzzed.

He stared at the screen.

Case 1701 was from twenty years ago.

The murder of Missy Johnson.

Emma stared at her chipped nail polish beneath Jordan's seeking gaze. "How is your dad?"

"Good." For the first time since his unexpected arrival, Jordan's smile was genuine. "He's got a condo in Clearwater, Florida. He's lost twenty pounds and visits the ocean every day. He's happy but he misses your mom. He misses you."

They'd all wound up back at Blanche's house after the fiasco at the police station. Emma had worried about all the extra people and commotion, but Blanche appeared to be in her element with the bustling activity. She'd ushered them into the kitchen and set out a carafe of coffee along with a plate of scones.

Emma searched for Liam, but he was nowhere in sight. There'd been no time to unearth her feelings and examine them. The shock of seeing Jordan at the police station had completely derailed her.

"I'm glad your dad is doing well. There wasn't much point in keeping in contact." Emma fidgeted with the chipped edge of her polish. "We're not related. I figured he'd want to move on."

Despite their rocky start, she'd grown to admire her stepfather as he'd cared for her mom during those last days. His selfless compassion had humbled her.

"We're family," Jordan said with a frustrated laugh. "You listed me as your emergency contact. That meant a lot to me. We must still mean something to you."

"Absolutely you do. I wasn't sure…" All her old insecurities came rushing back. No matter how many years passed, there was always a part of her that was ten years old and begging for approval. "Thank you for coming. I hope I didn't tear you away from anything too important," she added with a smile, hoping to alleviate the somber mood.

Meeting him at the police station while the cloud of a murder charge hovered over her wasn't exactly how she'd planned their reunion.

"I can hardly see straight." He pinched the bridge of his nose and scrunched his eyes. "I caught a C-133 cargo plane out of Kabul to get to Italy. Near froze my ears off on the way. Had to climb onto the crates looking for what little heat rose to the top. After that I caught a commercial flight. I flew overnight into Dallas, then I turned around and rented a car. I haven't changed clothes in nearly three days. I can't imagine how I smell. And I wouldn't have done anything different. Nothing is more important than you."

"I'm glad you're here. I'm glad you came."

He'd been a steady presence at her mother's funeral. Her stepdad had been inconsolable, and she hadn't fared much better.

"I wouldn't be anywhere else," he assured her.

"You were right about the house," she said, chucking him on the shoulder. "It's a real money pit, and I know absolutely nothing about home renovations."

Her amusement quickly dissipated. She'd never enter that house again without thinking of Artie's unseeing eyes.

Jordan squeezed her hand. "This guy is a sociopath, Emma. He's murdered someone. In your house. This is personal. This guy is icy, and that scares me."

Blanche appeared and gestured toward the staircase. "Your room is all ready, Mr. Harris. Let me know if there's anything you need."

"I most certainly will." He stood and snatched another scone from the table. "These are so light, I'm surprised they don't float away."

"Oh, go on." Blanche giggled. "I'm going to check on Duchess. Those puppies should be coming any day now."

As he passed Emma's chair, Jordan ruffled her hair like he'd done when they were kids. "Get some rest."

"I will."

He paused in the doorway. "I almost forgot. Lucy Sutton's husband passed away. An accident."

Lucy and Jordan had been friends when they were kids. Emma once thought they'd make a great couple, but Jordan was always traveling, and Lucy had married someone else.

"How is she doing?" Emma asked.

"I don't know," he said, his gaze focused on the distance. "We didn't keep in touch."

As Blanche and Jordan left the kitchen, Liam entered. He'd changed, and she realized she'd never seen him out of his uniform. He wore a plaid button-down shirt with the cuffs turned back. Some unidentifiable sensation knotted and tightened inside her.

He took a seat across from her. "It's nice that your brother is here."

"Yes."

Liam seemed different, though she couldn't quite put her finger on the change. He'd been distant and distracted since the police station. She recalled the telephone conversation he'd had before they'd discovered the body. Had someone given him bad news?

"I know I told you not to bother tracking down Jordan." She held up a hand to silence his protest. "But I'm glad you did. He's the only one I trust as much as you."

Liam didn't seem particularly pleased by her gratitude. He exuded a restless energy, his arms crossing and uncrossing before he bridged the distance.

"Don't put your trust in me." He grasped her by the shoulders before quickly letting go. Digging his heels into the floor, he shoved his chair backward. "I'm not what you think I am. Trust yourself. Trust your instincts. But don't trust me to protect you."

"Why not?" His abrupt flare of anger caught her off guard. "What if my instincts are telling me to trust you?"

"Then don't listen." His face was pale and his voice raspy. "Don't listen."

She seemed to go hot and cold at once. This man was a stranger to her, and she was more frightened than when she'd woken in the pitch darkness to frigid water rising around her. This forbidding and unapproachable man had her more lost and confused than ever. He was the one constant she'd had since the accident, and he was telling her not to trust him. Staring at his stony face was nothing less than torture.

"Okay." She'd meant to be strong, and instead she barely managed to get the word out. "Can you at least tell me what's wrong? Can you at least tell me why you're mad?"

"I'm not mad. I'm—I'm not," he said, his expression filled with anguish. "The timing is bad, that's all." He stood and rubbed his shoulder. "I'll do everything I can to protect you, but there might come a time when I'm not enough."

"You said we'd get through this together." Her muscles quivered, and she brought her clenched hands down to her lap. "And that's all I'm asking. Nothing more."

Where was the tender man who'd held her in his arms and comforted her?

"You should ask for more," he said, his agitated gaze conveying his impatience. "You should be demanding more. I'm not the man you think I am."

An icy calm crept over her. "Why are you even here then? If you have things to do, then go and do them. If you have someplace you need to be, then go there. I'll manage just fine without you."

A crushing ache tugged at her limbs. He'd been reluctant to take her case from the beginning. She wanted nothing more than a deep, dreamless sleep that lasted until this nightmare was over.

"I don't know how to explain this." He gathered the

plates from the table, his restless energy evident. "This is my fault." The dishes clattered. Bracing his hands against the sink, he hung his head. "I used to think that doing the right thing was enough. People still get hurt, though. Sometimes doing the right thing isn't enough."

"What else can we do? There are no guarantees of anything."

"I'm failing you," he said in a thick voice. "I'm failing you and it's tearing me apart."

"You only fail me when you turn away. I need you."

"I'm trying to protect you. Even if that means protecting you from me. What if I'm not enough?"

The truth humbled her. He wasn't angry with her; he was angry with himself. What secrets from his past had caused such a heavy burden?

As she stood and reached for him, she wasn't certain which of them she was trying to comfort. They were both lost and alone—facing an unknown enemy with few resources at their disposal. He hesitated a moment before crushing her against his chest. Relief rushed through her, and she knew she'd been lying to herself all along. She was greedy. She'd thought she could ignore his appeal, that she could set him on a shelf like a fond memory. She was wrong.

His scent was clean and masculine, and her emotions fractured. Her need was unquenchable. His embrace was strong and safe, and the only thing she was certain of right now. He held her as she trembled, infusing her with a sense of peace. He was physically powerful, and his strength was part of his appeal, but she'd never been afraid of him. She'd sensed his gentleness from the very beginning. Even before she knew herself, she'd been drawn to the kindness of his soul. He held her close without being threatening, offering only comfort.

He was the only anchor against a world that wouldn't stop spinning out of control, and she was desperate to regain her equilibrium. He stroked her back before threading his fingers through her hair. She rested her head against his shoulder, letting the fear and worry drift away as his heart beat strong and steady against her ear.

What if he turned his head ever so slightly and he kissed her?

Her pulse jumped frantically. He must feel as though the weight of the world was balanced on his shoulders. She'd meant to give him comfort and instead she was taking. What did she even have to offer? A guilty flush crept up her neck and she pulled away.

"Whatever happens," she began, struggling to find the right words. "Whatever happens, I'm glad I was able to know you."

With a suddenness that stunned her, he turned away.

"I feel the same," he murmured.

Emma gathered more dishes from the table, grateful for something else to occupy her hands and her thoughts. Liam joined her, and they bustled through the awkwardness. Together they cleared the table and loaded the dishwasher, carefully avoiding brushing too close together, and she was grateful for the reprieve.

"Your stepbrother has won over Blanche," he said, filling the silence.

"I hope you're not jealous," she said with a teasing grin. "Blanche clearly adores you. You're first in her heart."

His expression shifted. "I'm a poor substitute for her son, that's all. Even I can see that."

"Can't it be both? Can't she care for you even while you remind her of her son?"

"She's better off with Jordan," Liam said with a laugh that didn't quite ring as authentic. "His suits are nicer."

"You should have a little more faith in Blanche." Emma had been feeling good for most of the day, but as the stars twinkled in the night sky, the aches and pains from her accident came to the forefront. "You should have more faith in yourself."

The irony wasn't lost on her. Moments before she'd been wondering what she had to offer Liam. They both had moments where they felt as though they were obligations. The insecurity was universal.

Facing her, Liam caressed the yellowing bruise at her temple. "How are feeling? Any headaches?"

"No." A shiver traced over her skin where his finger touched. "A little battered from yesterday's adventure but recovering nicely. How about you?"

"My surgeon would have a heart attack if he knew what I'd done to my shoulder." His laugh was rueful. "But it's not so bad."

He retracted his hand and stared at his fingers, as though surprised by his actions.

Her senses filled with the details of him. Freshly washed, his hair contained a hint of wave she hadn't noticed before. She wanted to collect her memories of this time and tuck them away somewhere safe.

She sensed he'd known little softness or comfort in his life. He seemed uncertain of affection, surprised by it, almost, and her heart went out to him. She didn't feel pity so much as sorrow that he'd never been given the gift of unconditional love. Her compassion for him took precedence over any concerns about her own problems. He was haunted by a guilt she couldn't fathom.

As long as he kept the pain to himself, he'd never heal. He had to let go of his guilt in his own way. In his own time.

"When this is all over," she said, "how about we meet

for a cup of coffee like regular people without a care in the world?"

"That sounds nice," he replied. "I'd like that."

As she watched his retreat, she knew for certain there'd be no meeting for coffee. They barely knew each other, and he was already trying to tell her goodbye. Once he'd closed the case, she'd never see him again.

He said he'd only lied to her about his past, but he was wrong.

He'd lied to her just now. He'd lied about their future.

TWELVE

Liam absently rubbed the raised edge of the scar on his shoulder. Some days were worse than others. Some days he almost forgot about the injury, though the nagging ache never quite left. Other days, the pain battled for his attention.

Today had been a bad day.

He needed a little space. A little distance.

He'd spent most of his life as an outsider looking in. He'd spent the better part of his childhood in foster homes. In college, he'd commuted to campus rather than live in the dorms. While other kids partied on their parents' dime, he'd worked two jobs and carried a full academic load.

Dating had been a rare luxury, and something he'd looked forward to when the occasion arose. There was always that moment in the beginning of any new relationship when everything was possible. There'd even been that time he'd thought of proposing. Probably for the best that his girlfriend had broken up with him before he'd gotten up the nerve.

He'd thought creating a different future might erase his past. He'd been too young and naive to realize that no one ever really escaped.

Once he'd asked Jenny why she'd never gone to college. Why she'd never tried to break out of the old neighborhood.

I got black lungs, she'd said with a laugh. *You know how people who work in the coal mines get black lungs from breathing the air? That's what this neighborhood does to you. We all breathe the rotten air and it makes us sick. We all got black lungs from bein' poor.*

A square package resting on his nightstand caught his attention. He tore open the envelope and stared at the cover. *Killer Instincts.* Emma's book. He flipped it over and stared at her publicity shot. Her elbows were braced on a windowsill overlooking a narrow, wrought-iron balcony. She was glancing over her shoulder, as though the photographer had caught her in a moment of candid reflection.

Her eyes caught and held his attention. He'd come to recognize a familiar world-weary cynicism in the eyes of people who dealt with violence for a living. He'd seen it on the faces of the kids he went to school with, and he'd seen it in the cops he'd worked beside over the years. Once a person stared into the face of evil, they were never quite the same.

Emma had seen into that void.

He returned downstairs and discovered her asleep on the overstuffed sofa in the parlor. A book rested on the floor where it had fallen from her fingertips. He retrieved an afghan from the back of the couch and draped it over her sleeping form.

He'd been a jerk to her earlier because he didn't trust himself. Weathering strong emotions had never been a talent of his. He was more adept at loneliness. He took pride in his work. When sorrow threatened to overtake him, he boxed those feelings and stored them away.

Nothing in his life had prepared him for joy. For love. Sorting through his feelings for Emma was like writing a manifesto with his left hand. Everything felt awkward and clumsy. Retreating into anger had put him on familiar ground once more. He was falling for her and falling hard.

Their relationship was built on a faulty base. She didn't know him—she didn't know the real man. He didn't belong in her world. That was the problem with living the life he had—he didn't know where he belonged. When each day was a lie, truth became a luxury.

For the past six months, he'd been fighting his assignment here, fighting the town. Somewhere along the way, Redbird had gotten under his skin and become a part of him. He wanted to go fishing, and he wanted to take Emma.

Someone had shattered the sense of safety he'd taken for granted here, making this case personal.

Emma murmured something in her sleep and thrashed. He rested a hand on her shoulder, and she reached for him without opening her eyes.

An aching tenderness took hold of him. When she was near, it was impossible for him to put up a wall. He was drawn to her. He wanted to be the one person she turned to in times of trouble and in times of joy. Except they were all wrong for each other.

Emma was courageous, and he was a coward. He'd faced a loaded gun with less trepidation than this spirited woman. He'd rather take a bullet than be a disappointment in her eyes. She was worth the risk, but he didn't know if he had it in him.

Living in the fantasy was safer than facing the truth.

After shutting off the lamp, he gently closed the door behind him.

He stepped into the hallway and caught sight of a light shining from the kitchen. He discovered Mrs. Slattery sipping a cup of tea and reading the newspaper.

She glanced up. "How are you feeling? I was about to send up a search party."

"I just checked on Emma," he said, hoping his words didn't reveal the depth of his feelings. "She's fallen asleep."

"The poor dear. Don't wake her up. You both look like you could use a week of sleep."

"My thoughts exactly." He stifled a yawn. "Thank you."

"You don't have to thank me. I don't mind. It's all right, you know, to let people take care of you once in a while. You've been a real blessing to me these past few months."

"Remember when I told you that I was applying for a job in Dallas?" Though not the entire truth, the fabrication was close enough. "Looks like I might get a second interview. I'm driving up on Monday."

Her eyes widened. "That's short notice."

Shrugging, he said, "I can't pass up the opportunity."

As he contemplated a return to his old job, he braced for the familiar rush of anticipation. Instead, he pictured his apartment with its bare walls and plain furnishings. He thought about sitting in traffic on a Monday morning. He recalled the sweltering summer heat with no lake to cool the evenings.

Redbird was changing him in ways he wasn't sure he understood.

"I'll miss you when you're gone," Mrs. Slattery said mournfully. "But you know you can always come back to visit."

"You'll forget all about me as quick as a wink." He flashed a fake smile. "You won't even remember my face."

Her expression grew sorrowful. "Maybe instead of taking that interview, you should stick around here. There's a girl in the other room who's probably hoping the same thing, I'm thinking."

"I like her," Liam said, his face heating. "But the timing is all wrong."

I'm all wrong.

"I'll give you some advice. The timing is never right. I met my husband two weeks before he shipped out for the service. I didn't see him for another six months. If I'd waited for him until the timing was right, we'd never have been together. I'd just started a new job when I found out we were expecting Ben. Awful timing. I could go on and on and on, but here's what I'm trying to tell you—all of the best things that have happened to me in my life have happened at the worst possible time. Yet somehow some way, everything just manages to work out."

She was wrong. Timing was only part of the problem. If he stuck around here much longer, Emma was going to know he wasn't a hero—far from it. Once she saw through him, there'd be no going back.

"I'm glad I answered your ad," he said, uncertain how to put into words how much she meant to him.

She'd treated him like a favored son, and he'd enjoyed the experience.

"I am too. I don't imagine I'll keep the place up after you're gone. I'm going out of style, even for folks who are looking for a little nostalgia. Everyone prefers Airbnb these days. My website looks out-of-date, even to me, and I'm old. I can't keep up anymore, and I'm not sure I want to. Maybe I'll even sell the place. I've hung on too long because this is where all my best memories were made, but I can take them with me. Whatever I decide to do, you're always welcome in my home."

With a sudden shock, Liam realized this was the first place he'd ever lived that he didn't want to leave.

"I appreciate that."

She wouldn't say that if she knew that he'd spent the

past years lying for a living. He wasn't the kindly deputy she thought he was. She'd be shocked at the things he'd seen. He was a man whose lies had gotten someone killed.

Jordan appeared in the doorway. "What's our next move?"

Mrs. Slattery folded her newspaper and set it aside. "You two have business, and I have a soft pillow calling my name. I'll leave you to it."

Jordan had showered and changed into jeans and a pullover, his hair neatly combed. He didn't seem quite as prickly as he had before. Liam assumed his earlier temper had been a result of his fatigue and worry.

"All right," Jordan said, the command in his voice unmistakable. "Your dispatcher sent the case files to my analysis team. We're going to run everything through the system again. Not that I don't trust your guys, but we've got a deeper reach. None of this makes any sense. This guy plays out like a serial killer, but the evidence points to a cold case. When nothing makes sense, that means that something is missing."

"My thoughts exactly."

"Where do we go next?"

"We have to talk with someone. Deputy Bishop. He's worked for the county for over twenty years. He directed me to look into Missy's case. That has to mean something."

"What do you think of this guy, Bishop?"

"To be honest, we have to consider him a suspect."

"Noted."

"His brother dated Missy. If there's something to hide, he had the means and the opportunity."

"But he wants to talk to you about the case? That doesn't seem real smart if he has something to hide."

"Yeah. I know. I haven't figured out the angle yet."

Jordan slumped in his chair. "We'll have to bring Emma."

Liam sighed. "I know."

The other man braced his hands on his thighs, his fingers pointing at each other, his elbows jutting out. "I was hard on her when she moved here." He muttered darkly. "Who am I kidding? I've been hard on her since she took up writing about serial killers. After we found that body, I don't know… I can't explain it. I wanted to forget, and she couldn't. I thought I could bury all the feelings and forget it ever happened. Emma knew different. Sometimes I think I punished her for that. I punished her for making me deal with the pain."

Liam felt like someone had sucker punched him. He'd done the very same thing. He'd lashed out at her because she was forcing him to reveal parts of his soul he'd kept hidden.

"I know the feeling," he said.

"I'm sorry about this morning. I was an… I was a jerk." Jordan slapped his hands against the table in a quick drum riff. "Wouldn't it be nice if people only saw us at our best? I guess that's the thing about family. They know you at your worst but they have to like you anyway. Mostly because you've seen them at their worst, as well. Emma has her moments. Especially if she's hungry. I'd carry granola bars if I was you. It all balances out, I suppose."

Liam's world transformed, and he struggled to bring it back into focus. He'd never had the luxury of being authentic. Every home he'd lived in as a child had been a never-ending audition to stay another day. Any slip he made he risked getting bumped to another home.

Revealing his injury to Emma had been the closest he'd ever come to admitting weakness.

It had never once occurred to him that someone might

love him in spite of his weakness, yet examples abounded all around him. He'd been taught love and forgiveness in the Bible, the one constant he'd had in his life.

He'd practiced forgiveness with everyone but himself.

Jordan stood and slapped him on the shoulder. "Tomorrow we talk to this deputy. Tonight, we rest. If I don't get some shut-eye, I'm not going to be any use to anyone."

Liam spent the next half hour in contemplative silence. He'd lived his whole life by a rigid set of rules.

What if those rules no longer served him?

"Why did you want Liam to look into Missy's case?" Emma asked Deputy Bishop with a reassuring smile. "Have you discovered new evidence?"

They'd talked Bishop into meeting at the sheriff's station during the lunch hour, when the place would be empty. Jordan and Liam had come at the poor man like battering rams, and he'd immediately clammed up. Sometimes a softer approach was needed.

The station occupied the second floor of a brick building on Main Street, with a bank of windows facing the town square. The sheriff had his own office decorated with stuffed deer heads and pelts scattered over the wood floors, while Liam and Bishop had facing desks outside the lockup. The two opposite walls were exposed brick, while the outside walls had been insulated and covered in light paneling. The effect was rustic and charming.

Bishop scratched his ear. "I always get assigned the cases no one wants. The low priority stuff. Except some things shouldn't be low priority, if you know what I mean."

"I'm not sure that I do."

"I've been working here more than twenty years, and between the two neighboring counties, at least a dozen women have gone missing in that time."

"Wait a second." Emma gaped. "A dozen women? How can that be? Someone would raise an alarm if that many women disappeared."

"Not these women." Bishop lifted his shoulder in a careless shrug. "They're undocumented. When someone like that goes missing, no one looks real hard. Everyone figures they went back across the border or something."

"But you don't think so?"

"Nope. I've been following up on these cases for years," Bishop said, his fist bouncing against his knee. "Around here, we open a case, we ask a few questions, we let some time pass, then we close it out. I think there's more to it. Take that girl they found next town over. Everyone said she overdosed, but she had ligature marks on her wrists. Doesn't sound like drugs to me unless it's a cartel killing, and those bodies don't get found."

"Why are you bringing this up now?" Emma asked. "After all this time?"

The deputy glanced at Liam. "Because you're good at what you do. I used to be. I'm not anymore. I wanted to see if maybe you could look into it. Because only young, pretty girls without documentation seem to go missing. That can't be a coincidence. I brought it up to the sheriff when you said we might have a serial killer living around here. What if someone has been targeting these girls because he knows we aren't looking for them?"

Liam leaned against a desk, his ankles crossed. "What did the sheriff say?"

"He told me to keep digging."

"You mentioned the Missy Johnson case." Liam straightened and set his jaw. "Why?"

"Couple years back, a rancher found some bones on his property," Bishop said. "The crime lab identified the remains as a woman. Spanish descent. We get a tip that one of the cartel leaders, Reynosa, ordered the hit. Case closed. Except something always bothered me."

"What was that?" Emma prodded.

"The blue twine," he said. "The remains of the woman that was found on the ranch had traces of blue twine. Missy's hands were tied with blue twine. That detail stuck with me."

Liam and Emma exchanged a look.

"Did Artie ever ask you about Missy's case?" she asked.

"Nah. No one ever asks me about police work."

Emma kept her expression carefully neutral.

"You were around for Missy's case," Liam said. "What did you think? Did they get the right guy?"

"I thought so at the time. Now I'm not so sure. The guy who confessed got a lot of the details wrong. I brought it up at the time, but Sheriff Phillips was sure we had the right guy." Bishop slid his palms over his thinning hair. "Sheriff Phillips was on duty that night, but he stopped at a party over at the Eagle's Club. People were more open-minded about a fellow having a drink on the job back then. But after they found Missy, he didn't want anybody to know he'd been out boozing. He didn't want the papers back East painting him like some sort of drunk yokel."

Liam jotted down a note. "That was Ruth Garner's six-tieth birthday party, right?"

Bishop flicked his chin. "Let me see now. That sounds right. Yep. The sheriff's brother organized the party. Must have burned the sheriff when he did that. Those two were always fighting to see who was going to be their ma's fa-vorite. They almost came to blows that night. Phillips had to drag them off each other."

Emma patted his slender knee. "You've been very help-ful. I appreciate you taking the time to talk with us."

"Things are going to be different from now on. I want you to know that. These past two years, all I've been doing is speed traps and delivering warrants. I got bored, I guess. My mama always said that boredom kills more men than all the plagues and famines combined. A bored man finds trouble, she said. I guess I found me some trouble. I'm changing, though."

Emma looked at the deputy, really looked at him. He was thin to the point of emaciated, and his skin was sallow. Understanding finally dawned on her. Bishop was fighting an addiction. The deputy had been hiding his affliction well, but the physical strain was starting to show.

"Does the sheriff know?" she asked quietly.

Bishop grunted. "'Course the sheriff knows. He knows everything around here. He's helping me, though. Got me on the waiting list for a rehab center in Austin.'

Her heart went out to him. "Things might get harder before they get easier. If you need any help, you let me know. I'll keep you in my prayers."

"You do that. Prayers." His bark of laughter turned into a coughing fit. "I'm gonna need 'em."

Liam paced the distance between the holding cell and his desk. "All right. Let's think this through. Emma comes to town and stirs up interest in a cold case. Then Artie goes digging around and finds something. What if Bishop is right? What if it's all connected to the missing women in the area?"

Jordan braced one hand on the corner of Liam's polished oak desk. "Yeah, but if Emma knew the killer's identity, why did he let her live?"

"Because she didn't know his identity."

Emma threw up her hands. "I don't understand."

"You only had to rattle the guy," Liam said. "If he'd

gotten away with murder for this long, he probably wasn't worried at first. I think whatever Artie found pushed him over the edge."

Jordan nodded. "Which meant Artie had to be silenced. But since Emma had amnesia, he could continue to toy with her. This guy is sick."

"I've felt that since the beginning," Emma cried. "That this was a game to him."

"Wait a second." Jordan reached for a pencil. "The two obvious suspects are the brothers of the sheriff and the town deputy. That's a tangled mess."

"Don't forget the sheriff himself," Emma added. "Bishop said he was in town for the party. What if he's hiding evidence to protect his brother?"

"That doesn't make any sense," Jordan said. "Bishop claims they hate each other."

Something had been nagging Liam all week. A puzzle piece that was out of place. He took a seat before his computer and clicked through a few screens.

"Do you remember that first day at the hospital?" he asked Emma. "The sheriff said he'd given you a speeding ticket. Only the sheriff never runs speed traps."

He clicked through a few more screens and pushed back from his desk. "Nothing. He never gave you a speeding ticket."

"Why would he lie about that?" Jordan asked.

Emma leaned over him and grasped his shoulder. Her hair fell like a curtain, brushing against his cheek.

"If Artie was digitizing the articles," she said, "then there must a website someplace."

Liam clicked through a few more screens. "Got it. The Redbird *Gazette*. It's digitized through January 2015."

"That should be enough," Emma said, tapping her chin. "Run a search for Sheriff Garner."

A growing suspicion curdling his stomach, Liam typed in his first and last name. "There are over twenty hits."

Emma pointed at the screen. "Start here." He clicked on the link, and she read the headline out loud. "'Former Redbird resident loses wife in tragic boating accident.'"

"We thought he'd only been married twice but look at this. There's another death in his history." Liam toggled to another window. "It's an obituary from the Fort Worth newspaper. 'Former Redbird resident widowed after tragic accident.' That makes three wives. One disappeared, and two had tragic accidents."

His blood grew sluggish in his veins.

Emma shook her head. "That's a lot of tragic accidents for one guy. Blanche said his first wife ran off. What if she didn't?"

Liam didn't want to believe the sheriff was guilty because that made him a gullible idiot.

Emma had pulled out her phone and stared at the screen. "Sheriff Phillips died in a car accident. Garner became sheriff after a special election. That's a lot of dead bodies surrounding Garner's rise to power in the county."

Liam's head was spinning, and his vision collapsed inward. Everything fell into place. The sheriff had been playing them all along. He'd been working undercover right beneath their noses, using all the tricks of law enforcement at his disposal.

"Jordan," Liam said, catching the other man's attention, "check and see if Juan Reynosa is listed in the Department of Defense database."

All the evidence from the sheriff was suspect now.

For the next fifteen minutes, the three of them gathered articles from the Redbird *Gazette*. Sheriff Garner was a pillar of the community. He'd also benefited from a number of untimely deaths. On a hunch, Liam started searching for missing women in the neighboring towns. There were several requests for "welfare checks" over the years, many of them for women with Spanish names.

His heart pounded painfully against his chest. He'd taken a vow to protect and defend the people of his community. The sheriff had taken the same vow. This whole time he'd been dropping false clues, leading them in circles while he watched them chase their tails. He'd questioned Liam's relationship with Emma to throw him off balance. He'd degraded Bishop, calling him "Hopalong" to discredit the deputy.

Jordan disconnected his phone call with a shake of his head. "Juan Reynosa isn't in the system."

"Then Garner lied about the DNA."

"That's not all," Jordan said, his face grim. "There *was* a DNA hit on the bullets left at the hospital. Remember when I decided to run a second check on all the evidence in the case? There was a DNA match, all right."

Liam swiveled around. "Don't keep us in suspense. Who is it?"

"You."

THIRTEEN

The room descended into hushed silence.

Liam's breathing instantly became a painful experience. "Me?"

"Yep."

He forced his pulse to slow. He hadn't done anything. The evidence was planted. They were building a case against the sheriff.

Emma's hand touched his shoulder. She lingered there, then slid her fingers to the nape of his neck and gave a gentle squeeze. "Everyone here knows the truth."

The shock waves flowing through him eased at her words. He stretched his arm across his body and gently gripped her wrist. He understood now how she must have felt when her memories came rushing back. Sorting through the roller coaster of revelations was exhausting.

Once more frustration rode him. All the clues had been laid out neatly before them. All they'd had to do was look.

Jordan splayed his arms. "We have to proceed with caution. We don't have proof of anything yet. Let's all remember that."

"He's right." Emma's hand slipped from Liam's shoulder. "All of this is just coincidences and conjecture. The sheriff has a stellar reputation in this community. If we go around telling everyone he's a killer, there's going to be a backlash. He's smart. He's gotten away with murder for this long already. We have to build a rock-solid case before we go forward. How on earth are we going to manage that?"

Liam nodded his agreement. "We have to find proof."

"He's been one step ahead of us all along," Emma added. "We have to be careful."

He appreciated her concern. The task was destined to be overwhelming. "We start with Missy Johnson. That case had the highest profile, which means it had the most evidence. Let's run everything again."

Jordan grunted. "I doubt Garner has any DNA in the database. He's too smart for that."

"What about those online DNA kits?" Emma said, rapidly pinching her fingers together as she formed her thoughts. "You know the ones. You swab your cheek and the next thing you know, you have a brother in Poughkeepsie and your parents aren't talking. If someone in his family tree ran a search, we can trace the DNA from there."

"It's worth a shot," Liam said. "It'd have to be a close match. A cousin. Maybe his brother is in the system."

Emma hung her head. "I doubt he's alive. They didn't like each other. How long before Garner decided his brother needed to meet a tragic end? With his closest relative gone, Garner inherited the property. There'd be no family squabbles over the teacups or the silver. He's murdered to clear his path for years. His wives die when he meets someone new. The previous sheriff dies when he needs a job. His brother is conveniently absent when the family property is being divvied up. He's been doing this for a long time."

She had a valid point. Garner had friends. Who knew what evidence he'd tampered with, even before he had official access as sheriff. He knew the town and he knew the systems.

"Agreed," Liam said.

Without evidence, they were dead in the water. In order to catch Garner, they needed something airtight. The guy had survived this long without getting caught; he wasn't an idiot.

"Wait a second." Emma paled. "Where is Sheriff Garner now?"

"I'll find out," Liam said.

That's just what they needed—the sheriff interrupting their evidence discovery session when he was their prime suspect.

Since everyone was at lunch, Liam called Rose on his phone rather than broadcasting his interest over the police radio and risk tipping off Garner.

"Have you seen the sheriff today?" he asked.

"It's his day off," Rose said. "He had a truckload of mulch delivered to his ranch yesterday, so I'm guessing he'll be busy all day."

"Thanks."

There was a part of Liam that wanted to believe everything was simply a coincidence. The sheriff had taken him in and treated him like a son. The other part of him knew his suspicions were true. The sheriff had been dumping the throwaway cases on Bishop for years, all the while knowing they'd languish unsolved. He'd lied about the DNA evidence. He'd balked at relying on outside agencies.

Not to mention all the convenient deaths surrounding the man. One missing wife was unfortunate. A missing wife and two "tragic" accidents was a sociopath at work.

On a hunch, Liam searched the database for missing persons in Fort Worth during the time the sheriff worked there, except the list was too long. He had no doubt, though, that a fine-tuned search would turn up additional victims.

The realization sickened him.

He'd placed Emma in the sheriff's care. He'd endangered her because he was too blind to see the truth.

In hindsight, the evidence was shockingly clear. The sheriff had been playing all of them, a skill he'd perfected over the past twenty—maybe even thirty—years.

"Take Emma back to Blanche's," Jordan said. "I'm going to make a few calls and get us some help out here. We can't trust anyone local. For all we know, someone's been helping him cover his crimes all these years."

"No." Liam shook his head. "Not Blanche's. He knows she's been staying there."

Jordan gathered his keys. "If this guy is off duty, then stay here. It's the last place he'll look."

His head reeling, Liam turned to Emma. "I've suspected Bishop all along. Garner wanted me to."

"The best camouflage is misdirection."

Jordan paused at the head of the stairs. "Give me three hours and I can have a team here. We'll tell the sheriff they're here about Emma's case, and we need his input. While he's here, we'll search Garner's ranch. My guess, we're going to find those missing girls buried on the property. He wouldn't risk burying the bodies off-site if one of them had already been discovered."

"Okay," Liam agreed. "We'll hunker down here."

Jordan galloped down the stairs. The distant sound of the door slamming marked his exit.

Emma collapsed onto a chair. "He locked me in my hospital room that night. He knew Bishop was taking the next shift, and he locked the door. He knew I wouldn't blame him."

"He fooled us all," Liam said quietly. "At least we'll live to tell the tale."

"It's funny, isn't it? He told us he was a great guy, and

we all believed him. I remember liking him that first night and not liking Bishop."

Lost in his own thoughts, Liam nodded. He'd known the sheriff better. There'd been signs. The sheriff had preyed on their weaknesses, exploiting their insecurities for his own gain.

The door slammed again, and footsteps sounded on the stairs.

Emma cupped a hand near her mouth and called, "What did you forget, Jordan?"

A sudden premonition gripped Liam. He stood, positioning his body between Emma and the top of the stairs as he reached for his service weapon.

Sheriff Garner appeared, a twelve gauge shotgun in his outstretched hands. "I wouldn't do that if I was you, boy," he drawled.

Liam's hand hovered at his hip. He'd worn his bullet-proof vest today. The addition had been an afterthought. If he pulled his gun, he might survive the buckshot.

Making his decision, he reached for his weapon.

Sheriff Garner was faster.

The buckshot exploded against his chest, lifting his feet from the floor. He sailed through the air, catching a glimpse of the deer head the sheriff had mounted above the office door before his world went black.

At least this time he was certain the bullet hadn't gone through him.

Numb with shock, Emma sat in the passenger seat of Sheriff Garner's SUV, feigning a calm she didn't feel. Tears dampened her cheeks and she twisted her wrists, straining against the handcuffs.

"I would have preferred you died in the fire," the sheriff said from the driver's seat. "This makes things a touch more complicated. Figures. Been living in this town off and on my whole life, and that was the one time those volunteer fire idiots got it right. How'd you guys finally figure me out anyway? Your amnesia was a lucky break. Did you finally remember it was me in that pickup truck?"

"You said you gave me a speeding ticket, but Liam knew you never wrote them."

"They're beneath me." He sneered. "That boy was bound to be trouble. I never should have taken him on."

"What are you planning on doing?" she managed to ask.

"Well, I'm putting the blame on your boyfriend, ain't I? People like stories so we'll give them a story. It'll have to be a murder-suicide. Deputy McCourt tried to burn you alive at Artie's house, but he failed and nearly killed himself in the process. I suspected him and took you into protective custody. He followed us to my ranch and there was a confrontation. I don't want to spoil the ending for you, but McCourt doesn't make it out alive. I might even get injured in the exchange. Makes it more heroic that way."

Bile rose in the back of her throat. "It won't work. You already killed him."

"He ain't dead," the sheriff chortled. "He was wearing a bulletproof vest. I can always tell on the skinny guys. Bulks them up. Plus, I shot him with buckshot. He's probably not looking too pretty, but he's alive. And he'll come for you. It's in his nature. He'll come charging in like some stupid hero, and I'll take him out. I'll be the proper amount of shocked and sad at how he killed you and then killed himself."

"The death of a deputy will bring an investigation and a lot of attention." Fear seeped through her bones. "No one will believe Liam was involved in a murder-suicide."

The sheriff threw back his head and laughed, the sound

echoing through the SUV. "You don't know him at all, do you? The US Marshals had to beg me to give him a job. He messed up real good in Dallas, and the DPD don't want him back. Ain't no one gonna take the time to investigate that old boy's death."

She glanced away, refusing to be drawn in, but the sheriff was too invested in his narrative to quit.

"You heard about the girl," he said, goading her. "How he got her killed."

Emma remained stubbornly silent. She didn't know what had happened in Dallas, but she knew Liam. Whatever occurred wasn't his fault, but he was carrying the burden.

A sudden hope struck her. The sheriff didn't know about Jordan. He didn't know about Jordan's contacts with the Department of Defense. They might not make it out alive, but Jordan wouldn't stop until he knew the truth.

As her heart hammered against her ribs, the scenery changed. The vegetation thinned, and the terrain turned flat and uninspired. They passed cars, the sheriff tipping his hat with a wave, happy to be seen with a passenger in the SUV. It was all part of his story. The ease with which he'd planned her death nauseated her.

"I run this town. I have for twenty years," he said with a friendly wave to a vehicle passing in the opposite direction. "No one has any reason to doubt me." He chuckled. "You, on the other hand, aren't going to be missed. I kept tabs on you in that hospital. Not one visitor. Not a one. Not one call to the office looking for a missing person. You couldn't have made it easier on me if you tried, and I thank you for that. You two are a couple of misfits, and no one cares about them."

He didn't know her. He didn't know anything about

her, and that would be his downfall. The realization comforted her as the time ticked away. The ride seemed to last forever. The land grew harsh and desolate. Not a cloud marred the painfully blue sky.

She forced air into her lungs, willing herself to breathe normally. She had to stay alert. Liam was coming for her, and the sheriff was setting a trap. She had to find a way to warn him.

The SUV kicked up dust as they drove beneath an arch of intertwined antlers.

The ranch house at the end of the winding drive was long and low and painted a depressing shade of beige. There were three outbuildings in various states of disrepair dotting the property. He yanked her from the cab of the truck and dragged her up the front stairs. Two sturdy rocking chairs sat side by side, and he shoved her onto one.

"Now we wait." He spat into the dust. "This is going to be fun."

They didn't have to wait long. Soon, Liam's Tahoe appeared in the distance, a plume of dust trailing the vehicle. He parked about twenty yards from the house and got out. Her heart lodged in her throat. His shirt was shredded and bloodstained. He held both arms in the air, a shotgun clutched in his right hand.

When Liam was about ten yards from the house, the sheriff ordered him to stop. He moved behind her chair and she felt the cold press of his handgun against her temple.

"Lower your weapon," the sheriff ordered.

Liam caught her gaze. "Don't worry. I'm going to get you out of this."

"Like you did that other girl?" The sheriff cackled. "Looks like the past is about to repeat itself."

* * *

Liam had been expecting the sheriff's goading, and the barb went wide.

He kept his gaze averted from Emma. Her distress was a distraction he couldn't afford.

"Let her go," he called across the distance. "This is between you and me."

"Not hardly," the sheriff hollered back. "I got a score to settle with you."

"What would that be?"

"I know what you're trying to do," Garner replied. "You can waste all the time you want waiting for the cavalry to come and rescue you. That's what I want, too. I need an audience if this is going to work."

"Then humor me. Tell me about Missy Johnson."

"You wouldn't be recording me now, would you, son? No matter. I'll search you when you're dead. And I know you're not live streaming anything. Can't get internet this far out."

"Then you might as well talk."

"I killed her, if that's what you're asking. Missy wasn't my normal target. It was a crime of opportunity, you might say. I was in a bad mood that night and she was walking home all alone after a fight with her boyfriend. Didn't hurt that she was Grant Bishop's girl. He needed to be knocked down a peg or two. Knowing she'd still be alive if they hadn't fought must have haunted him all these years. She was worth the trouble, but I learned my lesson with that one. After that, I learned to hunt people who lived on the outskirts of society, because when those folks fall off the edge, no one pays them any mind. In America, all men are created equal. *In America.* Those words don't mean nothing across the border. It's the dirty little secret we all keep, isn't it? Now when the urge squeezes me, I pick someone God didn't create equal. That way no one looks too hard. The Rio Grande has saved me more than once. There are places in Texas where the grass has soaked up so much blood, I'm surprised the sap of those scrawny brush trees doesn't run red."

"Bishop cared. He looked for those women." A haze of fury clouded Liam's vision. "He was keeping files on those girls. I think he suspected you all along, but he didn't want to believe it."

"He didn't suspect nothin'. I only kept him around because he's easy to fool. He's got a drug problem that he spends all his time trying to hide. He's nothing more than a statistic. He'll be in rehab for a while after you're gone. Then he'll owe me. I've been setting you up to take the fall on this all along. But you probably already figured that out, didn't you? I'll make sure there's a dent in your truck to prove you ran her off the road. Your DNA is all over the bullets the killer left behind. All the trails are going to lead right to you. I been doin' this for years. I know how to fool people. I know how to lead the clues astray. But I'm keeping things simple with you. I'll show the proper amount of shock and sorrow with a little remorse because I didn't catch you before you killed this little lady. People will believe anything I tell them. I'm a fine, upstanding citizen, after all, and you're a stranger. Wait until someone leaks the news about what happened in Dallas on top of everything else. They'll probably dig you up again just to hang you."

"Why Emma?" He stalled. Jordan had hopped out of the truck about half a mile back. He was circling around for a clear shot. "Was she getting too close to the truth?"

The sheriff ran his fingers down her cheek, and she shuddered away.

Garner laughed at her misery. "Imagine my surprise

when I discovered that *she* was hunting *me*. She was digging up all the old case files. Then Artie sank his teeth into the project. I figured it was just a matter of time before someone started to put the pieces together. Figured I better stopper the leak, if you get my drift."

Liam glanced over his shoulder.

The sheriff chuckled. "We got another couple of minutes before someone shows, but I think it's time we wrap this up."

"How many did you kill?"

There was a good chance either one or both of them were going to die in the exchange. Liam wanted all the information he could pull from the man before that happened.

"Too many to tell you in the time we have." Garner yanked Emma to her feet. "You come on up here so I can set the scene for the officers."

"What makes you think I'll go down that easy?"

"Cuz you're too softhearted. I read it in your file. You was crying because that girl bled out from the bullet that should have killed you. I was counting on you going off all half-cocked. You don't want to see this little lady suffer. I can make her death quick, or I can make it ugly. Your choice. But I'm counting on you to save her any more pain."

A flash of metal caught the sun. Jordan was in place.

Time to make his move. "Then let's do this."

Emma tipped forward and headbutted her captor in the chest. His arms flailed and he fired, but the bullet went wide. A volley shattered the front window.

Garner threw his hands over his head and danced an odd jig. "What the—"

A second gunshot from Jordan splintered the door

frame, forcing Garner to scurry into the house. The front door slammed behind him.

Emma bolted down the stairs and slammed into Liam's chest.

He'd never seen a prettier sight. Garner had gotten sloppy in his panic, and he'd left his hostage behind. A fatal mistake.

His shotgun at the ready, Liam steadied her with a hand to her waist. "Stay low."

There was a shed about twenty feet from the house, and Liam made for the protection it offered. From his hiding place, Jordan fired off a few more rounds to give them cover. Emma's harsh breathing sounded between the volleys. The distance wasn't far, but fear had drained her resources. Liam pressed his back against the chipped beige paint flaking off the siding and tucked Emma against him.

Her whole body quaked, and he shifted his attention. Her eyes were wide, her pupils dilated and her breathing was uneven. Her chin wobbled.

"I thought you were dead," she said in a ragged whisper. "I thought he killed you."

An overwhelming wave of love surged through him. Disregarding their precarious circumstances, he caressed her chin and angled her face up. Then he lowered his mouth and pressed their lips together.

The kiss was meant to distract her from the danger, to remind her to focus on being alive. He wanted her to know that, no matter what, he'd get her to safety—even if that meant risking his own life.

She pressed her hands against his tattered shirt, feeling for the bulletproof vest that had saved his life. The warmth of her lips unleashed a tenuous hope he never thought he'd feel. He knew he was holding her too tightly, but for a moment, his arms refused to loosen.

Wresting for control, he pulled away, breaking the kiss. "We're going to survive this. Jordan is here. You'll never have to fear Garner again."

She glanced at the shotgun, then threaded her fingers through his free hand. "I trust you."

The three words shimmered in the air between them. He wanted to explain everything, to confess what had happened in Dallas, but this wasn't the time or place.

If she could love him at his best, then maybe—just maybe—she could love him at his worst.

Two more shots sounded, and Jordan jogged to meet them.

He pulled Emma into a quick, one-armed embrace. "You did good back there, sis."

"Thanks."

Jordan patted her hand. "We have a lot to talk about. How about we take out this guy and go home?"

"My thoughts exactly," Liam said.

A plume of dust caught his attention. "Someone else is coming."

They kept out of site until the familiar vehicle came into view. "It's Bishop."

Liam exited his cover long enough to wave the deputy toward them. Bishop angled his Tahoe between the house and their hiding place. He leaped from the cab, anchoring his hat to his head and staying low as he sprinted the distance.

"Good to see you, Bishop," Liam said brusquely.

"Not happy to be here," the deputy mumbled. "The sheriff is screaming over the radio. He says you've gone crazy and you're shooting up the place. When the Redbird police get here, you better lay low. They're liable to take your head off."

"Then we don't have much time."

"It's true, isn't it?" Bishop's expression was rigid. "He did it, didn't he?"

"Yeah. We're going to have to dig up every inch of this property. He confessed to killing Missy and the others. I'm guessing those women are here, somewhere, and they deserve a decent burial."

"I knew it," Bishop muttered darkly. "I didn't want to believe it, but somehow, I knew it. He's got the drop on just about everyone around here. Even me. It's like secrets and lies are his currency. He'll get you out of a jam, but then you owe him."

"He's going to answer for his crimes," Jordan said. "I'll see to that. But we have to get him first."

Liam assessed the situation. "Bishop, you stay here with Emma. Jordan and I will flush him out of the house." He motioned toward the porch. "You take the front and make some noise to flush him out the back. I'll be waiting."

"Got it," Jordan said, then took off without a backward glance.

Liam started to follow, but Emma snatched his arm. "Be careful. I can't go through that again. I can't... I can't lose you."

Pressing a hard kiss to her lips, he cupped the back of her head. "I'm going to finish this."

Liam skirted around the house, swiping the sweat from his brow. The back door faced the open range. There wasn't much cover behind the dips in the terrain and the patchy scrub. Garner had cornered himself.

Jordan fired off a few shots and hollered. Liam pressed his shoulder against the side of the house and watched the back door. An agonizing amount of time passed. Nothing happened.

"He's not coming out," Liam shouted.

"Then we'll take him inside."

The maneuver wasn't ideal, but the faint echo of sirens bolstered his courage. They didn't have much time, and he didn't want to be shot in the crossfire. Leading with his shotgun, he whipped around the corner and scanned the interior.

What he could see of the house was meticulously neat. The furniture was set at precise, right angles. There were no rugs immediately visible on the floor or pictures on the walls. The kitchen was on the left separated by a tall countertop, which meant the hallway on the right must lead to the bedrooms.

Jordan entered through the front door, and Liam crept through the backdoor. "Nothing."

Gesturing with his chin, Jordan said, "You take that way. I'll check the other side."

Liam nodded. His heart hammering in his chest, he kicked open the doors to three empty bedrooms and searched the closets and hiding places. He came up empty.

"Out here!" Jordan called. "I've got something."

Jordan had pulled aside a throw rug in the kitchen, the only floor covering in the house, near as Liam could tell, revealing a trapdoor.

As Jordan flipped back the covering, Liam aimed his shotgun at the opening. The other man peered into the void.

"It's an exit," he said. "A tunnel."

The same thought struck them both with equal horror.

"Emma," Liam whispered hoarsely.

FOURTEEN

Emma huddled behind the shed and rubbed her sore wrists. Bishop paced the narrow hiding place, his shuffling progress agitated. A bird fluttered past, and he drew his gun before laughing nervously.

"This is taking too long," he said, his body vibrating with tension. "I'm going to go check it out."

"They said to wait here."

Bishop shook his head with a quick, jerky movement. "Nah. I ain't waiting. I gotta see what's happening."

Her annoyance flared. She wasn't a weak woman, but she didn't appreciate Bishop leaving her in the lurch at every opportunity.

"Do you have an extra gun?" she demanded.

He guffawed. "What do I look like, a shop clerk? No, I don't have an extra. I got this one."

Pressing her hands against the side of the shed, she carefully peered around the corner. A thump vibrated beneath her fingertips.

"Did you hear that?" she whispered.

"No. What are you talking about?"

"Shh!" she ordered harshly. "I think there's someone inside here."

Bishop's returning glare was skeptical. Whatever he might have said was lost when the door slammed open.

Emma yelped and stumbled backward. The sheriff appeared before them, blocking their path to the house. His eyes were wild and unfocused. The tidy, controlled man she'd known before was gone, replaced by a snarling, disheveled animal. He swung his gun violently. Aiming first at her, then at Bishop.

"Get out of here, Hopalong!" he screeched. "Go back to your pills or your meth or whatever it is that's turning you orange. I can't believe you took a shot at me before. You almost turned into a man today. Almost. Don't make me kill you just when you're starting to grow a backbone."

Bishop paled. His expression turned blank, and the gun sagged by his side.

"That's right, Bishop, she's going to die either way," the sheriff snarled. "You might as well save yourself. Run along. The adults have business."

The deputy's shoulders slumped, and he turned.

Emma gaped. "Don't leave me."

The sheriff chortled. "Bishop is a coward. Always has been, always will be. Your boy isn't going to save you, either. He's going to watch you die, and I'm going to watch him fry for it."

Her ears buzzed, and she feared the paralyzing anxiety was going to consume her. He still didn't know about Jordan. He thought Bishop was the second shooter. She clung to that thin shard of hope.

The sheriff leveled his gun at her head. "I switched out the bullets. When they dig the slug out of your brain, they're going to trace it back to lover boy."

A red haze descended over her vision. She should have told Liam how she felt about him. She'd made some bad habits over the years—immersing herself in other people's tragedies had left her jaded and isolated. She'd buried both of her parents and spent her waking hours reliving the losses of others.

Her work had changed her, and she'd pushed her closest friends and family out of her life to concentrate on the dead. If only she'd recognized that every moment in the company of someone she loved was precious and worth fighting for. Love was worth suffering for.

Her dream came rushing back. The man in the ballroom holding a gun. The man she'd trusted. The man who'd betrayed her. That man was standing before her. A part of her mind had known he was guilty all along, and she'd been trying to warn herself.

She offered up a silent prayer of forgiveness for both of them. Cringing, she waited for him to pull the trigger.

The next instant there was an explosion. The sheriff jerked and fell forward, landing facedown before her.

Bishop stood behind him, a gun in his outstretched hand. "Guess he was wrong about me."

The sheriff was motionless, his neck cranked to the side, his eyes unseeing. The deputy had shot Garner in the back before he'd had a chance to pull the trigger and kill her.

Emma's knees gave out and she dropped to the ground.

The next few hours passed in a blur. She wanted to speak with Liam, to share her feelings, but they never had a moment alone. There were sirens and helicopters and police swarming the ranch. Throughout the entire ordeal, he never let go of her hand.

Bishop had shot Garner in the back. Texas law allowed the shooting since the witnesses on scene agreed with Bishop's reasonable belief that deadly force was necessary to prevent the sheriff from trying to kill Emma. The deputy had other problems that he'd have to take one day at a time. Emma sensed he was ready to face his addiction. He'd turned a corner.

The sunset was glorious, all things considered, a melting ball of orange slipping beneath the horizon. The sight reminded her that life was going on around them. She wasn't giving up what she did for a living, but she was going to make other changes in her life. She was going to dedicate as much time to the living as she did to the dead.

Liam cupped her cheek and brushed the hair from her forehead. "We should be able to go home soon."

"Can we go to Blanche's? Her house feels like home to me."

"Absolutely." He massaged her temple with his thumb. "How are you holding up?"

"Splendid," she said, inhaling deeply. "I'm alive and every day is a gift."

For the first time in a long time, she felt something glorious.

She felt at peace.

Liam woke early to the aroma of brewing coffee drifting through the house. He passed the dining room and discovered Emma watching over Duchess. She sat on the floor, a blanket draped around her shoulders. There were four tiny, squirming pups, each no bigger than his fist. Duchess proudly licked their heads as they blindly wriggled against her side.

Jordan had returned to work, but the siblings were planning a trip to Florida to see his dad—the ordeal had brought them closer together.

Liam rested a hand on Emma's shoulder, and she patted the floor. "Sit with me."

Folding his legs, he settled beside her.

She flashed a radiant smile, and he felt as though his insides had turned to liquid. "How are you feeling this morning?"

Touching his cheek, she said, "You can stop asking me that. I'm fine."

"I know. I guess maybe I'm asking to make myself feel better."

"Then I take back what I just said. Ask as often as you like if it helps."

Emotion clogged his throat and his nose pricked. "I have to tell you something. Something I should have told you a long time ago. I have to leave on Monday."

She turned to him, her eyes wide with surprise. "You're leaving?"

"I should have told you before, but I couldn't. My name isn't Liam McCourt."

Emma sucked in a breath. "I don't understand."

"My name is Liam McCallister. When the US Marshals put someone in hiding, they let you keep your first name and the first initial of your last name. Makes the adjustment easier, and if you're writing a check, gives you a chance to correct yourself." He barked out a humorless laugh. "Not that anyone writes checks anymore."

"Is this connected to your shooting?"

"Yeah." He ran his palms down his face. "But I didn't tell you the whole story. I grew up mostly in foster care. I was bounced around from home to home in a not so great part of town. I joined the Dallas PD and eventually worked my way into the gang unit. My superiors put me undercover because people knew me, but not well. I was safe. Except there was a girl. Her name was Jenny. We'd gone to school together as kids, but she didn't remember much about me. Her boyfriend was a member of the Serpent Brotherhood gang. One day he backhanded her. I came to her defense. It was instinct. I thought I played it off, but the guy was suspicious. He started asking around. Didn't take him long to realize that while I might have grown up in the neighborhood, I hadn't been active in any of the local gangs. That was enough to start unraveling my cover. Just like that he was holding a gun on me, yelling. Asking me if I was a cop. The next thing I knew, he pulled the trigger. He said it was a mistake. That mistake went through my shoulder and hit Jenny in the neck. Caught an artery. She bled out in minutes."

A gentle hand guided his chin toward her. "I'm so sorry. That must have been awful."

"Jenny's boyfriend went nuts. The scene was a mess. Swerve thought he'd killed us both. Dallas PD was running the undercover operation with the Feds, and they didn't want anyone to know the gang had been infiltrated. They didn't say a cop was involved. Instead, they said a civilian was killed and gave me a new name before sticking me here. It's not much of a hiding place, but no one was looking for me in the first place. They all thought I was dead." He pinched the bridge of his nose. "That's my story. She'd be alive if it wasn't for me. If I hadn't made a mistake."

He'd thought he was ready to face the unknown. He wasn't so certain anymore.

"I hate to break it to you," Emma said, a sweet, forgiving smile pulling up the corners of her mouth "But you're not the first person who ever made a mistake. You didn't kill Jenny, and you're not responsible for her death. A thousand choices led to that moment. The choice to defend Jenny was only one of them, and not even the most important one. She had the chance to change her life, just like you did, but she didn't."

"I know that now, I think, but her death will always be a part of me."

"That's okay, too. The dead will always be part of us. We simply have to remember to give as much attention to the living."

Getting that off his chest was like releasing a dead-weight. For a moment, he felt as though he might float to the ceiling if Emma hadn't been there to anchor him.

"What happens on Monday?" she asked.

"The Dallas district attorney is wrapping up the case. I have a deposition. Then it's over. I can go back to work. I can be Liam McCallister again."

"Is that what you want?"

"Well, here's the thing." Choked with emotion, he couldn't speak for a moment. "You like the person I am now, and I like that guy too. Except he's not the whole picture. But I thought, well, I thought that if you could love me at my best, then maybe you could love me at my worst, too."

She shocked him by covering his mouth with hers in an ardent kiss, stopping only when Duchess barked her displeasure.

Emma grasped his cheeks and pressed their foreheads together. "You sweet, lovable, adorable, *crazy* man. Of course I'm falling in love with you. You made it impossible for me to do anything else."

"You're not mad that I lied to you?"

"How can I be? You told me you were lying to me from the beginning. You couldn't even lie about lying."

"You don't mind the name McCallister?"

"It's growing on me. We can name one of the puppies McCourt. For sentimental reasons." She tweaked his nose. "If you want to move back to Dallas, I can work anywhere. And I want to sell my house anyway. I don't think I can ever live there again. I'm not cut out for a fixer-upper."

"Here's the thing—I'm not certain what my future holds."

She scooted to the side and rested her head on his bent knee, staring up at him with her brilliant topaz eyes. "I think we could both use a nice, long vacation to sort out the future."

"I know this great little bed-and-breakfast." He ran his fingers over the silken strands of her hair. "They allow pets. McCourt will have a place to stay, too."

"Mmm. Sounds nice."

"I'd like to stick around and finish falling in love with you."

"I'd like that too," she said.

"You should know that I'm kind of old-fashioned. I want a house and a couple of kids and a dog and a standing date at the dock at twilight when the fish are biting."

"Let's start with the fishing and work our way backward."

"Deal."

"You know, for the first time in my life, I finally feel at home."

His eyes misted. "Me too," he said. "Me too."

EPILOGUE

Emma adjusted the hanging sign that had previously advertised Blanche's Bed & Breakfast, then stepped back to survey her work. Months had passed since Sheriff Garner's shocking death, and a lot had changed in that time. Liam's testimony had been pivotal in the trial against Swerve, and the Serpent Brotherhood had splintered apart.

The porch door swung open and Liam appeared along with Duchess and McCourt, the puppy they'd adopted from the litter. Her heart fluttered. She could hardly believe they'd been married for nearly two months already. They'd initially agreed to date each other for a year to see if they suited. Their wedding ceremony had taken place only weeks later in Blanche's garden while the asters and the snapdragons were still in bloom. Blanche had already decided to sell, and though the house was far too big for only Liam and Emma, they'd bought it anyway. They had plans to fill up the extra rooms with children instead of guests.

Liam glanced at Emma's sign and groaned. "Do we have to put that in our yard?"

"Absolutely," she declared proudly.

She never tired of looking at him—of being near him. From the day they'd decided to marry, everything had fallen into place. They argued occasionally, both of them adjusting to a life that included two people rather than one, but they never stayed mad for long. He was still hesitant—

she sometimes caught him looking at her as though he feared she'd vanish into thin air—but he was gradually learning to trust in their love for each other.

He was gradually learning to trust in their future.

"Seems only fair we have something on display." Emma shrugged. "You are running for the office."

He'd been serving as interim sheriff and the time had come for the official election.

"Yeah," he said. "But I'm running unopposed. Hanging a sign in the yard seems like overkill."

Bishop had taken early retirement and moved to Arizona. The change of pace suited him, and he'd been sober since the shooting. Liam had hired a deputy to replace him, but the department was still short-staffed. Though occasionally jealous of the amount of time he spent on the job, Emma had taken the opportunity to work on a book detailing her discovery of the Lonestar State Killer's identity.

Liam was finally poised to hire a second deputy, which meant they'd have more time to spend together. A good thing considering what she'd discovered this morning.

"I almost forgot," he said. "Blanche sent a picture."

He scrolled through his phone and flashed the screen in her direction.

Squinting, Emma stepped forward. "Is she parasailing?"

"Yep. She loves Florida. She's going on a boat ride to spot dolphins this afternoon."

Though he'd never admit as much, Liam had worried that once Blanche relocated, they'd lose touch. Nothing could have been further from the truth. The distance had made the three of them appreciate each other all the more.

"And here I thought she was going to miss the old place," Emma said.

Liam wrapped his arm around her waist, and together

they gazed at the freshly painted Victorian house. "I think she was ready for another family to move into the house. And she'll be back this summer for the town's 150-year celebration."

"Jordan might visit, as well. He said he had some news. Can't wait to hear what it is. Summer will be an excellent time to visit," Emma said with a mischievous smile. "We might have—"

A friendly honk from a passing vehicle interrupted her words.

Chad, one of the volunteer firemen, leaned out the window of his truck and waved. "Say Liam, can I still count on you to help out with the pancake feed after church?"

"Wouldn't miss it," her husband replied.

Liam had not only embraced the town, he'd sewn himself into the very fabric of Redbird. They'd both worried about the reaction to the truth of his identity, but most everyone had embraced their interim sheriff and rallied around him. When the national news had swarmed the town with lurid headlines about a serial killer, Liam had provided a calm, articulate voice for the community. His efforts had earned him the respect of the locals.

Chad offered another friendly wave before turning onto Main Street.

"Don't be late," he shouted across the distance.

"See ya' there,' Liam returned.

Emma threaded her fingers through his. "I'm glad you finally joined the breakfast club at the church."

"I'm not." Liam rubbed his stomach with a grin. "Those pancakes are parking on my waistline."

"Speaking of waistlines—"

"Emma!" a voice called. "So glad I caught you this morning.

Mrs. Lineham strode purposefully down the sidewalk, her elbows pumping in rhythm to her steps.

She paused before them and marched in place, then checked her fitness watch before declaring, "The historical society decided to revive the Redbird *Gazette* with an online-only version. I hope you'll consider becoming a contributing writer."

"Thank you for thinking of me but—"

"Excellent. You were our first choice. You're also the only famous writer we have in town."

"I wouldn't say famous—"

"Gotta go." Mrs. Lineham checked her fitness watch. "My heartrate is dropping."

Liam chuckled. "I think you should start an advice column. I can see the tagline now." He splayed his hands. "'Emma Knows Your Secrets.'"

"No, thank you." She shuddered. "I'm done with secrets for a very, very long time. The next book I write is going to be something light. Maybe I'll even write a children's book. Speaking of children—"

Liam's radio crackled to life and Rose's voice sounded. "Unit 120. We've got a report of a steer blocking county road twelve between mile marker thirty and mile marker thirty-one."

"Ten-four," Liam replied. He dropped a kiss on Emma's nose. "Duty calls. Don't forget we're having dinner at the Eagle's Club tonight."

"I won't forget."

Sighing, she turned toward the sign once more. This was the price of being the wife of a law enforcement officer. There was always a small-town crisis interrupting them. And she wouldn't change a thing.

Liam's state-issue SUV was parked on the street outside the house, and he circled around the driver's side. "What were you saying about writing children's books?"

Emma turned. Steer or no steer, she didn't think she could keep the news to herself much longer. "The test was positive this morning."

Liam's head dropped out of sight as he bent to open the door. "What test?"

"Pregnancy test."

A car rounded the corner and honked. Liam was rooted to the spot. A dazed expression on his face.

"Oh dear." Emma rushed toward him and guided him toward the curb. "Are you all right?"

He stumbled slightly, then sat down hard on the curb, a lopsided grin on his face.

"Are you sure?" he asked, his voice hoarse.

"Not completely. It's early days. I haven't been to the doctor. Anything can happen."

He tugged on her hand, guiding her to sit beside him. "Are you happy?"

"Ridiculously so. You?"

"Same." He paused, the haunted look returning to his eyes. "I was afraid to pray for this, but I did."

Emma frowned. "Why were you afraid?"

"Because He's never answered my prayers before. I thought… I worried… I didn't want to hope."

Liam's past had left more than one stumbling block to their future, and she recognized the source of his doubt and insecurity. Jenny's death had left a scar on his soul.

"God always answers." She framed his face between her hands, and her heart turned over at the love she saw there. "But sometimes our prayers aren't in line with His will for our lives. That's why we have to trust in a bigger plan. Everything that's happened to us, both the good and the bad, has led us to this point."

"I love you."

He pulled her close and kissed her fiercely, and she recognized that he was trying to pour his heart and soul into the gesture. He was trying to tell her how much she meant to him.

"I love you, too," she whispered, then pressed her hands against his shoulder. "Now go. There's a steer blocking the road. Duty calls. We'll talk about this more tonight and for the next nine months."

He stood and helped her to her feet, then glanced at the sign swaying gently in the breeze. "You know, when you first suggested that slogan, I was skeptical. But I stand by those words. More than that, I take pride in them."

A flush of pure joy swept through her, and she pressed a hand against her stomach. Before she'd only hoped he was starting to trust in their future, but now she knew for certain.

"Liam McCallister for Sheriff," she read the words out loud. "A Name You Can Trust."

* * * * *

*If you liked this story from Sherri Shackelford,
check out her previous
Love Inspired Suspense book:*

No Safe Place

Available now from Love Inspired Suspense!

*Find more great reads at
www.LoveInspired.com*

Dear Reader,

When I first started writing, a mentor encouraged me to tape a picture of a "reader" to my computer to remind me of the most important part of the story—you. The reader is the most essential contribution to any book. Writers only provide the framework; your imagination does the rest. Now when I sit in front of my computer, I know I'm writing for Terrill, Valri, Debra E. and Trixi. I'm writing for Marnita, Bobby, Vernell and Cathy... I'm writing for you. I hope you enjoyed Liam and Emma's journey!

I love connecting with readers and would enjoy hearing your thoughts on this story. If you're interested in learning more about this book or others that I have written, I have more information on my website: sherrishackelford.com. I can also be reached at email: *sherri@sherrishackelford.com*, or at PO Box 116, Elkhorn, NE 68022.

My sincerest gratitude for being the reason I'm able to do what I love each day!

Sherri Shackelford

COMING NEXT MONTH FROM
Love Inspired® Suspense

Available November 5, 2019

SWORN TO PROTECT
True Blue K-9 Unit • by Shirlee McCoy

K-9 officer Tony Knight's best friend and unit chief was murdered—but he won't let the same thing happen to his friend's widow, Katie Jameson, and her newborn daughter. With the killer on the loose again and stalking Katie, Tony and his K-9 partner will risk everything to stop him.

SOLDIER'S CHRISTMAS SECRETS
Justice Seekers • by Laura Scott

Jillian Wade's husband was supposed to be dead, so she's shocked the special ops soldier just rescued her—and the daughter he didn't know existed—from gunmen. Now she and Hawk Jacobson must unlock his fragmented memories before the enemy strikes again.

HER FORGOTTEN AMISH PAST
by Debby Giusti

When Becca Troyer is rescued in the mountains by Amish farmer Ezekiel Hochstetler, she remembers only two things: a bloody knife and that she's being targeted. Will recovering her forgotten past prove fatal...or can Ezekiel shield her?

DEADLY CHRISTMAS PRETENSE
Roughwater Ranch Cowboys • by Dana Mentink

Posing as her twin sister is the only way to save her, but Maggie Lofton needs help. The only person she can turn to is her sister's cowboy ex-boyfriend, Liam Pike. But can Maggie and Liam work together to face down danger... even as they fight their feelings for each other?

HOLIDAY MOUNTAIN CONSPIRACY
by Liz Shoaf

After his last CIA mission ended in treachery, Nolan Eli Duncan holed up in his remote mountain cabin, preparing to trap his betrayers. But when journalist Mary Grace Ramsey is shot on his property while trying to reach him, he must protect her from a conspiracy deeper than either imagined.

DANGEROUS CHRISTMAS MEMORIES
by Sarah Hamaker

After witnessing a murder, hiding in witness protection is Priscilla Anderson's only option. But with partial amnesia, she has no memory of the killer's identity. When Lucas Langsdale shows up claiming to be her husband right when a hit man finds her, can she trust him to guard her from an unknown threat?

_____

LOOK FOR THESE AND OTHER LOVE INSPIRED BOOKS WHEREVER BOOKS ARE SOLD, INCLUDING MOST BOOKSTORES, SUPERMARKETS, DISCOUNT STORES AND DRUGSTORES.

LISCNM1019

Get 4 FREE REWARDS!

We'll send you 2 FREE Books plus 2 FREE Mystery Gifts.

Love Inspired® Suspense books feature Christian characters facing challenges to their faith... and lives.

FREE Value Over **$20**

YES! Please send me 2 FREE Love Inspired® Suspense novels and my 2 FREE mystery gifts (gifts are worth about $10 retail). After receiving them, if I don't wish to receive any more books, I can return the shipping statement marked "cancel." If I don't cancel, I will receive 6 brand-new novels every month and be billed just $5.24 each for the regular-print edition or $5.99 each for the larger-print edition in the U.S., or $5.74 each for the regular-print edition or $6.24 each for the larger-print edition in Canada. That's a savings of at least 13% off the cover price. It's quite a bargain! Shipping and handling is just 50¢ per book in the U.S. and $1.25 per book in Canada.* I understand that accepting the 2 free books and gifts places me under no obligation to buy anything. I can always return a shipment and cancel at any time. The free books and gifts are mine to keep no matter what I decide.

Choose one:
☐ **Love Inspired® Suspense**
Regular-Print
(153/353 IDN GNWN)

☐ **Love Inspired® Suspense**
Larger-Print
(107/307 IDN GNWN)

Name (please print)

Address   Apt. #

City   State/Province   Zip/Postal Code

Mail to the Reader Service:
IN U.S.A.: P.O. Box 1341, Buffalo, NY 14240-8531
IN CANADA: P.O. Box 603, Fort Erie, Ontario L2A 5X3

Want to try 2 free books from another series? Call 1-800-873-8635 or visit www.ReaderService.com.

*Terms and prices subject to change without notice. Prices do not include sales taxes, which will be charged (if applicable) based on your state or country of residence. Canadian residents will be charged applicable taxes. Offer not valid in Quebec. This offer is limited to one order per household. Books received may not be as shown. Not valid for current subscribers to Love Inspired Suspense books. All orders subject to approval. Credit or debit balances in a customer's account(s) may be offset by any other outstanding balance owed by or to the customer. Please allow 4 to 6 weeks for delivery. Offer available while quantities last.

Your Privacy—The Reader Service is committed to protecting your privacy. Our Privacy Policy is available online at www.ReaderService.com or upon request from the Reader Service. We make a portion of our mailing list available to reputable third parties that offer products we believe may interest you. If you prefer that we not exchange your name with third parties, or if you wish to clarify or modify your communication preferences, please visit us at www.ReaderService.com/consumerschoice or write to us at Reader Service Preference Service, P.O. Box 9062, Buffalo, NY 14240-9062. Include your complete name and address.

LIS20